For Better, For Worse?

By

K.F. Coffman

ISBN: (Paperback) 0-9766-2604-7
ISBN: (Hard Cover) 0-9766-2605-5

Library of Congress Control Number: 2006900961

This book is printed on acid free paper.

Printed in the United States of America
Carter Lake, IA

K.F. Coffman Publishing - rev. 01/04/06

Dedication To My Grandchildren

To my first, Kaycee, my first granddaughter, you are my little angel. You touch my heart in ways I never knew possible. You show me new ways to love each time you take my hand in yours. You were named after me and will always have a special piece of my heart. Grandpa loves you so very much now and always and will forever be with you in your dreams and heart, I Love You Kaycee, my little "doorknob."

To my second granddaughter Lynise, through your eyes I see all things are possible, dreams come true and the land of Oz is real and Dorothy will live forever. You can light up a room with nothing but your smile and your laugh is like the songs of Angels. I will love you always and be in your heart and dreams forever, we will never be apart. Grandpa Loves You more than words can say "Dorothy."

To my third grandchild, first grandson, Dylan, you are pockets full of dirt, puppy dog tails, turtles, frogs and worms. You make me laugh and show me that through your eyes the world is a wonderful and exciting place to be in, especially with you in it. You make my heart soar and complete my life in ways I never knew possible. Grandpa Loves You now and always and will forever be with you in your heart and dreams "Tin Man."

To my two new granddaughters Aalyce and Alexcia, you have brought new joy to my life and showed me just how exciting and new the world can be with two rays of sunshine like you both in it. You are new to our family but will be in my heart always. I will be in your hearts and dreams always and Grandpa Loves You both very much.

To my brand new, yet to arrive grandson DaKota, I want to say that Grandpa is very anxious to meet you. You like all the rest will have a very special piece of my heart and will allow me to see all the wonderful things life has to offer through new eyes. I will be in your heart and dreams always and will love you for all eternity.

Special thanks to a very special lady that I love like my own. You helped with ideas, you took the picture for the cover and inspire me in ways you couldn't imagine. I love you Erin.

Chapter 1

Sunlight flooded the neatly kept kitchen from the dawning of a glorious new summer morning. Birds were singing their morning serenade and it was a picture perfect beginning to a wonderful new day. The dainty but tasteful kitchen sheers were gently swaying to and fro from a gentle summer breeze and the smell of freshly brewed coffee lingered in the air.

First appearances would lead one to believe that a somewhat older couple lived here. Everything neatly decorated and in its place would support this. Looking past the kitchen would further support the first impressions with family portraits lining one wall in the living room, and again, nothing out of place or cluttered.

Outside, this tiny white frame house with adorable blue shutters on every window, would reveal a perfectly kept yard. It even had a somewhat manicured appearance and was clear that the owners took pride in their tiny home. Flowerbeds were many and summer blooms abundant.

Looking around the outside would reveal a very well kept garden and patio area in the rear. Although the flowerbeds in the garden area needed some attention as weeds had nearly taken them over. The tiny house almost looked out of place in the neighborhood as vast sprawling homes surrounded it. Nonetheless, it was immaculately kept and had an almost serene appearance amidst the much larger homes around it.

It was evident that the neighborhood sported many families and children. Bikes and scooters and numerous toys scattering the neighboring lawns would support this assumption. Even in this somewhat early hour children's laughs could be faintly heard from nearby homes.

It appeared to be a picture perfect summer morning and nothing would ever lead one to believe that this wasn't what paradise might look like. The sky was crystal clear, not a cloud in sight, and the sun was almost blinding. Although it was still somewhat early, the temperature was rapidly climbing and it would prove to be another hot summer day in Iowa.

Back inside the tidy little home one would find an unexpected sight. It was a sight that would leave most dumbfounded as the first impressions you would get from the home would never prepare you for what was inside.

He sat at the kitchen table sipping his coffee and stared out the window into nothingness. Wondering how he ever got to this point in his life. His marriage had been on the rocks for a while, but he never saw himself alone and starting over. They had been married for more than twenty-five years and though it lacked more than it contained at times, he always thought they would tough it out.

Now here he was, fifty years old, disabled, broken hearted, lost and alone. Trying desperately to put what pieces he could of his life together again. Nothing seemed to make sense anymore, nothing seemed to matter. If it hadn't been for his children and grandchildren, he would have given up all together.

They were the only things in his life that gave him the courage to wake and face another lonely day. Today would be no exception, another empty day starring out the window into nothingness.

As he sat and reflected back on what had happened, and how, one thing kept coming to mind. He blamed himself for all that had happened and he knew that was wrong, very wrong. It wasn't his fault, not entirely anyway.

Nonetheless, he couldn't shake the feelings of guilt that overwhelmed him at times like this. He always felt like he could have done something differently or worked a little harder to make things work out.

Maybe if he hadn't overlooked and ignored the warning signs, he could have fixed things before they got so out of control. As he reflects back, he can see everything as clearly as if it were only yesterday. Maybe it was just easier to tell himself that she wouldn't do anything as terrible as what he suspected her of.

Like most people faced with the harsh reality of your spouse cheating, you try to look the other way and tell yourself that it can't be happening to you. He was no exception. He denied to himself and his family that his beloved wife would ever do anything so awful. Yet deep in his heart he knew the truth. He knew that all the unspeakable things he imagined were real, very real.

Today would be no different from any other. He would dredge up the past, dwell on it and blame himself for everything. As he recalls all the dirty little details, he hangs his head and lets the tears flow. It is such a sad sight to see this big, strong man break down like a child and weep uncontrollably. "Just another day in paradise" he thinks as he wipes the tears from his eyes and saunters over to refresh his nearly empty coffee cup.

He glances at the calendar as he pours himself a fresh cup of coffee and realizes that just over a year has passed since his divorce had been declared final. "My God, it has already been more than a year" he mumbles to himself as he wanders aimlessly into the living room to turn on the televison. "Maybe some sound in this empty place will take my mind off things" he mumbles to himself.

Flipping through the channels and deciding that nothing really interests him at the moment, he takes his cup and heads out the backdoor. Maybe some time in the yard will take his mind off things, if even for only a short time.

He knows that he has to quit dwelling on the past and things he can't change. His wife has moved on and started a new life with her lover. Yet, he couldn't bring himself to go forward with his own life. That was something he just wasn't ready to do just yet.

In his mind he thought that moving on and starting over would finalize things and there could be no chance of reconciliation. He knew in his heart that getting back together was not something that was likely to happen.

Yet, he just couldn't turn lose of that last shred of hope. He knew that his ex was happy and had stayed with the man he had caught her cheating with. She had no problem moving on and he knew that it was more than time for him to do the very same thing. Still, he just couldn't bring himself to do that.

Just how do you close the door on something that has been such a huge portion of your life? In fact, he had been married to this woman his entire adult life, and, didn't know that life even existed without her. They married much too young and everyone that knew them gave them no more than six months before calling it quits.

It was safe to say that reaching a milestone like their twenty-fifth anniversary quieted most of those critics. There were a few though that still didn't give them much chance of staying together even after all that time. In his mind, those critics were wrong and nothing would have made him change his mind at that point.

It saddened him deeply to look back and have to admit that they had been right all along. He refused to see it coming even though some close to him warned him over and over again to open his eyes and take a good look at what was going on. Maybe he was just too close to the situation and couldn't have seen it, no matter what had happened. They say that hindsight is twenty-twenty and in his case it seemed that this was more fact than fiction.

He places his coffee cup on the patio table, slides a chair out and takes a seat. As he sips from his cup, his thoughts unwillingly keep wandering back to the events that brought him to such a terrible point in his life. Events that eventually found him alone and bitter, to a point.

"How could she have done this to me?" he keeps repeating in his mind. He could understand it if he had been unfaithful himself or was an abusive husband. But, those things couldn't have been further from the truth.

He was attentive, loyal, loved her deeply and wouldn't have cheated on her had his very life depended on it. He worshiped the very ground she walked on in fact. He had been more than a bit distant since the injury that left him unable to return to work. For that he blames no one but himself. He also blamed the distance that he had put between them as one of the very factors that drove her to look for companionship outside their marriage.

Companionship was one thing, but, she took things further, much further. She was the one that made the fateful decision to share a bed with another man. She chose to take the chance and toss caution to the wind, just to get what she felt she wanted and needed. At least in her mind she got what she wanted and needed. He just hoped that she could look back now and say that it was all really worth the cost. For it cost her more than just her marriage, much more.

After it all became common knowledge to friends and family, she lost respect and maybe even a little of the admiration they all felt for her. Their children, although all grown and on their own, couldn't believe that their mother could do something like this. They distanced themselves just a bit.

He made sure that first and foremost they understood that no matter what had happened, she was their mother and would always love them. They all knew that, but, that didn't change the fact that they felt some sort of loss on their part for what she had done.

Looking back he could understand their point of view, but still made an effort to keep her a very big part of their lives. No matter what she had done, he didn't believe that she deserved to lose her children and grandchildren over it.

She had made what he felt was the wrong choice and some bad decisions, but, she was still a part of their lives and always would be. He did his very best to make sure his children and grandchildren knew this as he reminded them almost daily.

He also knew in his heart that his ex-wife appreciated his efforts. She had thanked him numerous times for inviting her to family events and holidays. Those were the hardest times for him, to see her and know that it was really over. It killed him inside each time he watched her walk out the door knowing she was not going to return.

It was as if he relived their breakup over and over each time he saw her leave. Yet, he also couldn't bear the thought of her not being included in such things. It was his decision to hide his feelings and pain just to make sure she remained a very big part of their lives.

Several of his friends told him repeatedly that he was a much bigger person than he gave himself credit for. They told him that they just couldn't do it. Some even went as far as to say that they would have done everything possible to keep her away from such things.

Just to give her a taste of the pain and suffering he goes through daily, if for no other reason. He just couldn't bring himself to be vindictive to her like that. Sometimes he wondered if it was false hope that makes him do it or just some sort of strange commitment that he still felt toward her.

Whatever the reason, he went out of his way at times to include her in happenings and to make her feel like nothing had ever happened. He couldn't bear the thought of her experiencing any of the pain and emptiness he felt almost daily.

All he ever really wanted was for her to be truly happy. Even if it meant letting her go to be with her newfound love, he was willing to do it. And, he would smile all the while and never come right out and let her know just how badly he was hurting on the inside. Although, he was pretty sure she knew.

He wasn't about to lay some sort of guilt trip on her or play some sympathy card to convince her to come back to him and work things out. If she ever did come back to him, it would be of her own accord. Not out of pity, sympathy, or guilt on his part.

He didn't want her sympathy, all he ever really wanted was her love. He stood fast on that decision. If he was to ever get another chance with her, it would be because they both realized just how wrong they had been. Not because she felt sorry for him.

He was feeling sorry enough for himself that it more than made up for the both of them. He was suddenly snapped back to reality from the ringing of the phone. He looked at the caller ID. Something he found himself doing constantly lately. Almost from desperation that it would be his ex calling, but, it was one of his friends.

Chapter 2

"Drag your sorry tail off that couch and come join us for breakfast" his friend said as soon as he answered the phone. "I'm not on the couch and my tail really isn't that sorry to tell you the truth" he quickly replied.

They talked for a while and only after convincing his friend that he had no intentions of ending the world, or himself, they said their good-byes. He decided to do something in the yard today and went back into the house to pour a fresh cup of coffee and put his old tennis shoes on.

As he sat and tied his shoes the phone rang again, thinking his friend decided not to take no for an answer, he quickly picked up and said "I've already had breakfast and I'm fine." "That's good to know dad but I wasn't calling to see if you had eaten yet" his oldest son, Kyle, said.

"Sorry buddy, I thought you were someone else" he told his son. It was quickly discovered that his son was inviting him over to his house this weekend for some fishing and a cookout. Kyle thought of himself as quite the backyard gourmet and Ted always like spending time with him and the family.

"I promise not to try and fix you up this time" his son told him. Something all three of his children did on a somewhat regular basis lately. It seemed that one of them always had a neighbor or friend or a friend of a friend that they were trying to line him up with.

He really loved his children but hated them trying to fix him up with dates all the time. He just didn't feel that he was ready to start dating yet. And, was bashful in expressing to them that when he was ready, they would be the first to know.

To tell you the truth, most of his friends were as bad as the kids when it came to trying to fix him up. They too always had a friend or a friend of a friend or distant relative or someone to line him up with. He loved them all dearly and wouldn't have been able to do all this without their friendship and support. He just wished they would all get the hint that he would start dating when he felt he was ready to. He knew that in time he would have to get out of that stuffy old house and start dating again. He didn't want to live the rest of his life alone, that much he was certain of. He constantly caught himself looking for Elaine.

Always listening for her whenever he did something. He still found himself waking up and patting the empty spot beside him in his bed and falling asleep waiting for her to miraculously walk in and turn down her side. But, she never did and he knew she wasn't going to either. He knew that when he was ready to finally let go, he would stop doing these things.

But for now, he just wasn't ready to let go and give up hope. Shaking off the wandering thoughts, he quickly accepted his son's invitation. He was actually looking forward to getting out and loved to fish. So, this might be just what he needed he thought. He hadn't seen his son and daughter-in-law in a few weeks and wanted to see his grandchildren as well. All in all it sounded like a fun weekend.

As soon as the details were worked out and what time that his son would pick him up agreed upon, they said their "I love you's and goodbyes." He had never been afraid to tell his children just how much he loved them and every conversation ended with an "I love you." He always prided himself on that and did it to this very day.

His parents had never really been big on outwardly showing emotion let alone express it verbally. It wasn't that he felt he wasn't loved as a child, just some things went unspoken. He was the total opposite with his children and was glad he had chosen to be that way. He continued to do it to this day.

He felt that maybe in some small way his children had grown up a bit more secure and stable because they always knew that they could express themselves freely. All three of his children had grown up knowing that they could come to him and tell him anything. Even if it meant they might be in some degree of trouble for it, they knew they could tell him everything. He shared a very special relationship with his children. Something you rarely find these days.

Most of his friends' children barely spoke to them and he was happy that his children were so open with him. Some of his friends had even told him that they were envious and maybe a bit jealous of the relationship he had with his children.

To this day, his children still include him in everything and still call for dad's opinion. He was proud of that fact and their love and openness toward him had been the driving force that had kept him sane for the last year.

If it hadn't been for the three of them, not to mention his grandchildren, he would be a total mess. He was a big enough mess as it was. Reflecting back like he was now didn't help. As a matter of fact, it only seemed to make things worse.

He just had to stop doing this every time he turned around, he silently thought. It didn't do him, or anyone else, any good to keep dredging up the past and going over it in his mind.

He quickly cleared the unpleasant thoughts and images from his mind and set about busying himself in his flower garden. They were in some dire need of attention since he had been neglecting them lately. He usually prided himself in a beautiful yard with colorful blasts of fresh blossoms everywhere. Lately his poor garden looked more like the weeds had taken over and he just sat back and let them.

He quickly sat about the task of pulling weeds and clearing debris from his flowerbeds. After a couple of hours in the yard he was more than a little ready for a much needed and deserved break. After all it was fast approaching lunchtime and his growling stomach was demanding attention.

He stood back and admired just how good the yard looked with only a couple of hours of work. The flowerbeds were clean and weed free. The yard was trimmed and mowed and looked spectacular again. He knew that it was now time for a much deserved break.

He always took great pride in making anywhere he lived look like he made an effort. Too many places anymore just looked like people could care less. He was definitely not one of them. Even the neighbors had enjoyed watching him over the last couple of years and

For Better, For Worse?

his transforming an otherwise bare and lifeless yard into a showplace he could be proud of. He worked hard and his rewards were well earned.

As he brushed himself off and grabbed his empty coffee cup, he wiped his feet and headed into the kitchen to wash his hands. After he was satisfied that his hands were clean, he started taking things out and sitting them on the counter. Not really sure what he was hungry for, he just started taking things out and stood back to look over the mess he had accumulated on the counter.

Trying to figure out just what could be made from the mess, took less time than he thought and soon he was sitting down to eat. After lunch he put everything away that needed to be put away and tossed others into the trash. He wasn't sure just how long some of those things had been around and decided it a safe bet to just dispose of them once and for all. With dishes done, food put away and old unsure of items in the trash he walked to the living room to watch the noon news.

It seemed to be the same news as yesterday, just some of the names had changed and locations were different. The weather was soon on and he watched for the weekend forecast to see if fishing with Kyle would be good or a washout. It was forecast to be a beautiful weekend with no rain in sight.

That would be a nice change of pace to get out, see the kids, and do some fishing as well. He was suddenly looking forward to this weekend. It would do him good to get out of the house and put unwanted memories behind him for at least one day.

It would give him some much needed time with his grandchildren too. He hadn't seen them in a couple of weeks and missed them immensely when he didn't. Kyle and his wife Erica, had three children. Two boys and a little girl.

His oldest, Mandy and her husband Dan, had three children as well. They however had two girls and a little boy. His youngest Tommy and his wife Debbie, had two little girls and were hoping for a boy on their next try. Tommy told his dad that with his luck he

Page 10

would have another girl.

With the three kids and eight grandchildren his life was as full as it could be at the moment. Full with exception that he always though his wife would be there to enjoy outings like this with him. Well, his ex-wife as was now the case.

That still took some getting used to on his part, even if it had been over a year already. Calling Elaine his ex-wife. Even though times had gotten quite tough between them since his accident at work, he always thought they would work through it.

Then again, he couldn't have ever foreseen the fact that she would take up with another man and eventually leave him for that man. Even after all this time he still found it unthinkable. She never gave anyone the impression that she would even think of doing anything like this.

All her friends were taken back by her actions and decision to leave Ted as well. They just couldn't believe she was the same person. She just wouldn't do anything as terrible and unspeakable like that. She shocked most of them when she did all this.

Ted knew that he was the one that drove a wedge between them after his accident but also thought they could work it out. After a while, Elaine just acted like she didn't want to work it out. He was certain now as he looked back, that she had already made her mind up to be with her newfound love Lou, at that point. Why else would she become so cold and distant so fast? It stunned the family, her friends and everyone that knew her.

Once again, Ted took the blame for everything that happened because he was the one that shut her out in the first place. When the doctors told him that he would not be able to ever work again, it changed him as well. He wasn't as attentive and understanding as he could have been or should have been.

He still didn't think that was reason enough for her to cheat and find someone new. They had been through tougher times than this and always worked them out. Why was this time so different he constantly asked himself? That was an answer that he may never get.

He just chocked it up to the fact that the kids were all grown and on their own and him and Elaine was finally alone. Maybe she needed more than he gave and that's what drove her to someone new. Whatever the reason, he was more than sure it was his fault and he could have fixed it if he had just worked harder at it.

Instead of wallowing in his own self pity over the accident, he should have drawn closer to her for support, not driven her away. Whatever the reason it was too late now and dwelling on it wouldn't change the fact that he was alone.

Chapter 3

Ted and Elaine married much too young. He was nearly 21 and she was barely 17. The fact that she was pregnant and underage made her mothers decision to intervene and push the issue of marriage a lot easier. He of course rapidly agreed with her mother, probably more from fear of what she might do legally if he didn't.

Besides, he could always just divorce her and go his own way should things not work out. And, most were betting that they wouldn't work out. He and Elaine decided to at least give it an honest try and go from there.

It hadn't been a smooth or easy road to say the least. They had their problems just like everyone else. Some were compounded by the fact that he was young and liked to drink a bit too much. They both did things they weren't proud of and even they thought more than once about just calling it quits and going separate roads. They decided to fight and make it work instead and he was never sorry that they had made that choice.

As soon as their daughter was born, Ted went through a day and night transformation and everyone was so proud of him for it. It was as if the birth of their daughter changed his life forever and gave him the courage to grow up.

With the arrival of their first son he seemed to be even more grounded and level headed and when their last child came along he was more husband than any woman could ask for. He had done it on his own and Elaine was so proud of him for it.

He loved and adored Elaine and those close to the couple said he worshiped her. He would have given her the world had it been within his grasp. He never abused or mistreated her and wouldn't even give being unfaithful to her a second thought. He was as close to being the perfect man as a woman could find and Elaine knew that she was lucky to have him in her life.

They did most things together and usually if you saw one of them, the other wasn't far away. They weren't wealthy or well off by any stretch of the imagination, but, when it came to love and a healthy family, they were rich beyond dreams. They lived, laughed and loved to the fullest and shared everything, good or bad. They lived in a small but modest home and knew what if was like to make a dollar stretch on more than one occasion.

They took great pride in their home, their yard, and even their vehicles were always clean and looked newer then they actually were. They were complete opposites yet the perfect match. Elaine had a temper that could make the devil himself duck and run for cover and Ted was more the calm, cool and collected type.

Elaine wasn't afraid to scream, yell and fight like a sailor. Ted usually just said "yes dear" and went along with her until she calmed down and he could reason with her. Although reasoning with her was sometimes a task not worth taking on.

The complete opposites, yet the perfect fit. They complimented each other so beautifully and others were both envious and jealous at times. Ted was tall and thin with a dazzling smile, long blonde hair and mesmerizing blue eyes. Elaine was tall for a woman and thin built with flowing blonde hair, crystal blue eyes and a smile that could light up the world. Of course that was when they were much younger. Before time, surgeries, injuries and gravity took its toll on them both.

Even today though Ted stood six foot two and weighed a hefty two hundred thirty pounds. He still had those mesmerizing blue eyes but his hair now had more grey in it than blonde. He wasn't obese by any stretch of the imagination, but he did have a spare tire now. Again, a product of age, injuries and gravity.

Elaine was almost five foot eight and somewhat tall for a woman. She still had the flowing blonde hair and the blue eyes that could stop a man dead in his tracks. She was still slim and could and did turn heads wherever she went.

Elaine of course was one of those women that aged very gracefully and never looked her age. Ted on the other hand, wasn't as fortunate, and most guessed him to be even older than he actually was. The fact that he had experienced several injuries along the way that would have left most crippled didn't help either.

He always fought his way back though. Even after his doctor told him he would never again be able to do certain things, he fought to prove the doctor wrong. He was one of those people that just doesn't stay down for long. He was never much good at taking no for an answer and would move heaven and earth to prove you wrong if you told him he couldn't do something.

Like Elaine, he was not one to be told he couldn't do something and would do his best to show you he could. As a matter of fact, Ted knew that the quickest way to get Elaine to do something was tell her she couldn't do it. She would go to her grave trying to prove that she not only could, but would do it. Again, the perfect fit and they complimented each other so beautifully most of the time.

They always shared things, good or bad, and talked to each other about everything. Even if one of them was sure an argument was sure to follow, they at least talked about it. They went almost everywhere together and Elaine was as much a part of holding the family together as he was.

She too was always fast with an I love you and talked to her children about everything. They of course came to Ted first but they always knew they could talk to their mom about it as well. Ted was kind of the "go to" guy and mom was the trusty standby.

As a matter of fact, Elaine was more like the kids' best friend and he was always more like the level-headed dad figure. Elaine was full of mischief and fire and could wear the kids out most of the time. She was kind of like a six-year-old on a sugar high without a nap most days. She was more than a handful most times and was everything he could ever hope for or want. The perfect fit, till it all came apart.

They weathered some very rough times in their marriage and most thought they would toss in the towel and call it quits. That just wasn't something that either of them was very good at, giving up. They worked harder than some and loved deeper than most and worked through some things that were sure to doom even the best relationships.

A lot of people close to them wondered how they seemed to make it look so effortless and always work things out. More than one couple they knew fell by the wayside and ended in divorce and were on their second or third marriages, but not these two. They just seemed to work it out and got stronger for the effort and hard work. Most of their friends envied them for what they had built over the years.

Ted used to tell people, "don't tell me happily ever after doesn't exist, it does if you want it to." He and Elaine seemed to be the proof of that until that day the announcement came that Ted would be moving out and they had filed for a divorce.

The couple had kept it pretty much a secret until it was to the point that it could no longer be concealed. That was Ted's idea, he wanted to shed the best possible light on Elaine and didn't want anyone thinking ill of her for what had happened.

As a matter of fact, a lot of those closest to the couple really never did know the real reason they split up. Most thought it was Ted that decided to leave and he let them keep right on thinking it too. He wasn't about to air their dirty laundry in public.

He didn't want people outside their inner circle that knew all the facts, to look down on her for what had happened. Even right up to the end he took the brunt of the load of blame and never told anyone what had really happened.

This distanced some from him but Ted always felt that if they were that petty in the first place, those were friends Elaine could have. The true friends stood beside him and most just knew that there was far more to what had happened than Ted was making common knowledge. They were true friends and just accepted this and respected his feelings and privacy and never pried.

It was these very same friends that had helped him in ways they may never realize when it came to dealing with everything and moving on with his life. As much as he was willing to move on anyway. Most of them figured a lot of it out when Elaine started publicly dating someone new.

Most knew that she was not the type to move on so quickly and figured that the new man in her life was a big part of the downfall of her marriage. None of them would ever come out and say anything, mostly out of respect for Ted, but deep in their hearts, they knew.

Some found it hard not to take sides and that was the last thing Ted wanted. He did not want their friends drawing lines in the sand, so to speak, and taking his side or hers. He really hoped they would just accept things as they were and remain friends to both of them.

Unfortunately, that wasn't the case, some drew that proverbial line and sided with him anyway. He was a smart enough man to know that real friends were hard to find and knew that he couldn't control their feelings and emotions. So, he accepted their friendship and didn't worry about whose side anyone took. He was just grateful that they chose to support him.

He also knew that they were all going to believe what they wanted to believe no matter what anyone said. After all, Ted did go out of his way to make it look like all of this was his fault. He didn't want to shed any kind of blame on Elaine. He still couldn't put his finger on why he should even care about how she looked to everyone, but he did then and still did today.

He couldn't bear to have anyone think ill of her so he did what he always did, took the brunt of it all and never told his side of things. This was just the way he was and most of his closest friends already suspected that the breakup was more Elaine's fault than anything Ted ever did anyway.

Most of the closest friends were the very ones that told him to wake up and see what was really going on in the first place. They could see what she was doing even if he couldn't or refused to see it. These were the same friends that stood back, never judged or said a word and just supported him as best they could. They were a bigger help in getting through the toughest part of this mess than they would ever know. Words couldn't begin to express how fortunate he felt to have these people stand beside him.

He just figured that the "fair weather friends" that sided with

Elaine were friends he probably was better off without anyway. He wouldn't swear to it, but honestly thought that a couple of them sided with her because they themselves were cheating. You know what they say about birds of a feather flocking together. He was glad they weren't people he would really consider friends anyway and thought himself better off without them in the first place.

He accepted things as they were, was happy these friends were still a part of his life and let the rest work itself out along the way. It was all he could really do in this situation and was just grateful to escape with any friends at all. He was almost certain that the biggest majority of them would blame him anyway and support her.

He didn't give them any reason to side with him as he was the one that left and for all intents and purposes, he shouldered the blame. They would find out the truth in the end he told himself and didn't worry about who sided with whom. He was glad for once that he was wrong and they stood beside him after all.

Chapter 4

Ted worked construction and Elaine was a stay at home mom and wife and loved it that way. She loved to shop and do things around the house. She was always building something or helping Ted with weekend projects. It seemed she caught his love of building things and soon was as good as any man Ted had on his crew. She could build almost anything and he was so very proud of her for always at least trying.

She was never one of the "Barbie" types that whines and cries about how they can't do something because it's a mans job. She would be the first to roll up her sleeves and get as dirty as any man he knew. She even tackled most minor auto repairs on her own and soon was a master with a wrench or circular saw. As long as she had her "map," actually a blueprint, she would attempt to build a barn, and actually did build a barn style shed once.

Ted, like any other working in a field like his, sustained minor injuries. Mostly cuts and scrapes, nothing too serious though. He did suffer a few broken bones along the way but no more so than the average person in daily life. He always said you can walk in the park, step in a hole you didn't see and break an ankle, that's just life. He had his share of scrapes, cuts and bruises but nothing major or life altering.

Their two boys had inherited their father's love for building and talked often about going into the construction field as soon as they were old enough. Elaine took great pride in the fact that the boys wanted to follow in their fathers footsteps. She was very proud of him and was proud to see the boys want to be like him. He was as close to the perfect man that she would ever find and she never doubted that.

He always supported his family, took time out of a very busy schedule to make time for them and loved them all without reservation. She always knew just how lucky she was to have him in her life and did everything she could to show him that. With lots of hard work and determination on both of their parts, they had a nearly storybook life together.

Days would find Ted on a construction site somewhere, barking out orders and inspecting work in progress. Elaine made the most of her days shopping for needed items, working in her yard or doing something with the kids. She was always the one on the front lines cheering them on in soccer, softball or anything they decided to participate in. Even when times made it impossible for Ted to be there, she was always there for the both of them.

It was as perfect a life as most of us would ever want to lead and had no end in sight. They were for the most part the perfect family and most that knew them marveled in their successes. Most of their friends envied them and some, where even jealous of them.

They were the perfect couple with the perfect family that all of us know from somewhere. Birthdays, Holidays and Anniversaries where always a large production for this family and friends were always present to share in them all.

Ted and Elaine both were very outgoing, friendly people that never hesitated to help a friend or family member in need. They were always the first to offer help and the last to leave when you needed them. Even their children had inherited their parent's love and devotion to family and friends and were extremely popular. And had friends over all the time. Most said they should have a revolving door on the front of their house with kids and friends in and out all the time.

Their daughter Mandy, the oldest of the children, was more like Elaine's best friend and sister and was always doing something with her mom. She was tall and thin like Elaine and had her mothers deep blue eyes and flowing blonde hair. She was also the biggest daddy's girl in the world and knew she could get her way with Ted anytime she wanted to. She was popular, had tons of friends and was one of those kids that sleeps through class and gets straight A's.

She loved school and working with kids and they always knew that she would end up doing something in either child care or teaching. She was the level-headed one like Ted and was the one people could depend on in time of need. She was full of life and loved to laugh and couldn't love her parents more or respect them more. She went out of her way to always at least try to do the right thing and her parents couldn't be prouder of her.

The middle child, Kyle, was the little comedian of the family and could always get a smile and laugh from you no matter how serious the situation. He was taller than his dad at six foot four and stockily built like Ted. He had his fathers blue eyes and blonde hair and was a handful. He was a bit of a rebel like his mom and although he really never got into any serious trouble, he was the one the phone calls from the principal referred to. He was mouthy and defiant like his mother and had a temper that could almost match hers. He was the first to attempt a dare and the one to call from the emergency room from the final results of that dare.

Although not a straight A student, he did well in school and loved and respected his parents with all his heart. He was also the first to see just how far outside the boundaries he could step before the real trouble began. He loved to push the envelope and was more of a risk taker like Elaine than a calm and collected person like his dad. He always had lots of friends and was all in all a good kid, though some thought him to be the trouble maker of the family.

Their youngest Tommy, was born premature and had some health problems from the very beginning. Nothing serious of life threatening, but enough to scare Ted and Elaine out of their wits. They even had to leave him in the hospital for nearly two weeks after his birth and Elaine was nearly out of her mind during that time.

He was always the little bookworm and had an IQ that would rival Einstein's. He could have stayed at home and not even gone to school and still had a 4.0 GPA. He always tried harder than the rest to prove he could do things and settled for nothing less than perfection in everything he did. He was more serious than the rest and was the thinker and problem solver of the family.

He was excellent in sports, made friends with anyone he came into contact with and loved his parents more than most kids ever think of.

He was a daddy's boy and respected his father, and loved him like nothing most has ever seen before. He was six foot two like his dad and built solid as a rock. He was a heartthrob to most of the girls and had his dads blue eyes and blonde hair. He would fight to the death for his dad and no one ever said a bad word about his dad. For that matter, no one ever said anything bad about any of the family because he was the first to defend everyone to the end.

He was a walking encyclopedia and knew everything about everything. If you ever wanted an answer to something, just ask him. If he didn't know the answer, and that was a rarity, he would find it for you, and it would be right. He was an amazing kid and they loved him with all their hearts.

The children, like all other families, had their moments. Mandy always thought the boys were much too young to hang out with her and her friends and soon found little brothers to be more pests than anything else. Of course the boys knew this and that made them even closer and more determined to make her life miserable whenever they could. Nothing ever mean or hurtful, just little brothers being all they can be.

The boys were pretty much inseparable and if you found one of them, the other couldn't be far behind. They loved sports and were good at anything they tried. They took great pride in embarrassing their sister anytime they could and would fight to the end to protect her. They all loved each other even though most of the time it went unsaid. They were always there for each other and everyone just knew that they would be close their entire lives.

Ted and Elaine both grew up in Iowa, Council Bluffs to be exact. It was a thriving, growing, prosperous town on the Missouri river in Western Iowa. Although not a sprawling metropolis, it was a major city in Iowa and a great place to grow up and raise a family. In their younger days, nights would find them both cruising Broadway, the major street through the city, and just hanging out with friends.

Parking lots were always full of carloads of kids and the local drive in restaurant was one of the most popular sites on the street.

Radios were always tuned to the same station and the drive in was always busy with orders of hamburgers, fries and Pepsi. It was a much slower time when the business owners actually looked forward to Friday and Saturday nights and the carloads of kids it would bring to their establishments.

Normal horseplay and foolishness were the most mischief that most ever partook in and the business owners were pleased to have them. Everyone was friends for the most part and just out to be with friends, have some laughs and good food. It was a much easier time than the times they raised their children in.

The city had grown to nearly twice its size and still growing. Broadway was now off limits to kids and cruising, and, business owners now thought the kids to be more nuisance than profit. So, they outlawed their parking lots to the kids. It was harder for them to find anything fun or productive to do and some sadly turned to more serious mischief than anything Ted or Elaine had ever seen. It was a small enough town to know your neighbors yet large enough to get lost in.

Still, it was a place that Ted and Elaine had called home their entire lives and were proud and happy to raise their children there. It was like any other place one calls home. It has its bad points right along with all it's good points. And, it's a place they loved and would raise their family in, without any doubts. With the growth of the city, jobs were always plentiful for the most part and Ted was never wanting or looking for a way of supporting his family.

The growth also brought plenty of new shopping opportunities for Elaine and she was not about to complain about that. She loved to shop and the new malls and shops the city's growth brought in, was a welcome sight to her. Ted couldn't help but laugh, "she could find a place to shop in the middle of Siberia" he told friends.

Chapter 5

Time marched on and soon Mandy was in high school and thinking about life after school. She was also dating and driving. Something that scared Ted to death, and the boys were talking about cars as well. They were all growing up so fast and before they would realize it, they would be all alone, just the two of them. It would appear they would come full circle. They started off just the two of them and soon it would be just them again.

Times like this find you with mixed emotions and Ted and Elaine both was going through each and every one of them. You hate to see your kids grow up and find their own paths in life, yet, you can't wait for the freedom it gives you at the same time. Like having the best of both worlds. Things you put off due to raising children were now a realizable goal. Trips alone, maybe a cruise, the possibilities were endless.

Of course they would have to wait and see if finances would allow them such luxuries when the time arose. Iowa winters are normally very tough on jobs like Ted's. He had been with the company long enough to secure inside work during the winter, but the weather was sometimes harsh enough that even those paychecks were a bit sparse. They had always planned ahead and he had saved what he could. They were never frivolous in their spending but also knew they could not afford to send their three children to Ivy League colleges either.

When the time came for Mandy to think about college, they would work it out. At least they would have several years in between kids as Mandy and Kyle had a three-year age difference. The difference between Kyle and Tommy would be less as they were only two years apart in age. They would just be getting Kyle settled into college and almost immediately have to start thinking of Tommy's graduation. That would be a bit tougher they knew.

They both always hoped the kids would want to go on to college. Ted had always thought about going but marriage and a quick family only seemed to make that impossible. He never regretted marrying

Elaine and loved his children dearly, so college just never meant that much to him. Elaine had never been one to want to go to college and was more than happy just being a wife and mom.

That was something Ted always felt a little guilty about. In the back of his mind he always thought he deprived her of the opportunity. She was quick to tell him she didn't want to go to college in the first place.

Ted always thought that if any of them would pass on the chance to attend college, it would be Kyle. He seemed to share his mom's lack of enthusiasm about going to school for another two or four years. Whatever happened, Ted would do what he always does, do his best for his family.

He was always the one that would go without for himself to see that Elaine and the kids got what they needed first. He always put them first and always would. When it came to his kids' educations, it would be no different. He would eat saltine crackers every day for lunch if he had to, to allow them the chance at a college education.

Elaine noticed it right away and as the kids got older they also noticed that he would say he didn't need anything when they went shopping. They would watch him wear his old socks till they couldn't be worn any longer before he would let Elaine break down and buy him any. But that's why she loved him like she did, he always put them before himself, always.

She knew that he would do without for himself so she and the children could get what they needed. As the kids got older, they noticed too and they were always telling him to stop doing that. He just told them that he had everything he could ever need with her and the kids in his life.

They could do nothing but love, respect and honor a man like that. Willing to go without to provide for his wife and family. That was the one thing that Elaine was always sure of, she could count on him no matter what. Times like this only made him more sure that they had made the right choice and worked to stay together. It seemed they both were better people for it and even their children seemed more rounded and secure because they did. Something they could be proud of no matter where life ever took them as a couple or as individuals. They made the right choices and their rewards were more measurable than one could imagine.

Soon Mandy was graduating and as expected, she graduated with honors. Her party was loud and everything she could have hoped for, her dad made sure of that. All her friends and family were there and even her two brothers were on their best behavior.

An event like this would normally be fair game to them and they would have done whatever they could to embarrass her. Not this time. They were both proud of their sister and acted like perfect gentlemen the entire day. Much to the surprise of everyone.

As Ted assumed, Mandy was soon getting literature on colleges and the application process was fully underway. Letters of acceptance and scholarships were rolling in faster than she could sort them out. Elaine did her best to help and they sorted through all the messes faster than everyone thought they would. Elaine was right beside her daughter with every college visit and every interview. She was great and Mandy was so happy to have mom with her to help with the really big decisions.

Before he knew it, or was ready for it, Ted was helping his little girl pack all her belongings in her car and sending her off to college. She had picked a school in Iowa and would be only an hour and a half from home. He and Elaine both just knew that meant mom doing laundry and seeing her every weekend.

They were ecstatic. Even the boys hugged her and both had tears in their eyes as they watched her pull out of the drive. It was apparent that they would miss her, even if neither of them would admit it.

It seemed like only days, even though it was several years later, Mandy had her Associates Degree and Kyle was graduating high school. Mandy decided to stay in school and work toward her Bachelor Degree in teaching and as expected, Kyle announced that he would rather work with his dad than attend any more school.

After talking at some length about it, they decided that the decision had to be Kyle's. He assured them that he felt right about the decision and told them he felt he could learn more on the job than through any book. Ted of course knew exactly what he was talking about even if Elaine did have some concerns.

Ted got his son a job with the company he worked for and Kyle was learning fast. He was soon one of the best workers they had and was highly thought of in the company. It was really apparent that he could have a future if he chose to stay with the company and pursue it. Ted laughed and teased Kyle by telling him that maybe someday he would be calling his son boss. Although they both laughed at the comment, Ted knew that it was more attainable than his son might think.

It happened before they knew it, but time had sped away from them like a runaway train. Mandy was graduating college with her Bachelor Degree and Tommy was graduating high school. It was a very busy spring that year and Ted and Elaine both were proud parents indeed. It was almost like seeing them for the first time all over again. Their babies had grown into adults and that could only mean they were getting older.

Mandy returned to Council Bluffs with not only her degree but with a fiancé as well. She had been dating a really nice guy all through college and Elaine always told him one day soon he would be giving his little girl away. He shuttered at the thought as most dads probably do, but, he also knew she was right.

Mandy got a job immediately at one of the local elementary schools and was soon living her dream of teaching and working with kids. The kids she taught just loved her and the school thought of her as the perfect find. They couldn't be prouder of her.

Tommy dropped a gigantic bombshell on the family with his announcement to enter the military instead of attending college. And of course Tommy being Tommy, he was fully prepared with outline, bar graphs, perspectives and a proposed twenty year outline of his future that most CEO's of any Fortune Five Hundred company would find it hard to argue with. It would have been comical had it not been their son's future they were discussing.

He of course made some very valid points and had more than a convincing argument to any protest his parents could present. He told them that he did in fact want to pursue a college degree and still work in the construction related fields. He quickly found that the Navy offered some of the best construction related training available in their Sea Bee's training courses.

The military would also allow him to obtain a college education without it costing his parents anything. He concluded by explaining that in the military, he could attend the finest schools and obtain degrees in Engineering that he would only be able to dream about any other way. Ted and Elaine both knew their son was right, even though neither of them wanted to tell him that.

He was very convincing to say the least, and, he was also eighteen and could make this decision with or without their blessing. A point he made as a last resort. He only hoped they would support him in his decision and be happy for him.

They of course were both happy and proud of him, yet more than a bit concerned. Any parent has to have concerns when their children tell them that they are joining the military.

They reluctantly agreed to support his decision and watched him board a plane for boot camp with both pride and sorrow. The entire family was in tears as they watched his plane taxi out for takeoff. That was the first night that he and Elaine talked about the fact that they were finally alone again.

It was just the two of them, just like they started out so many years ago. They both found it saddening and yet somehow exhilarating at the same time. For the first time in what seemed like ages, they had the entire house to themselves and it was quiet.

With Mandy living just across town and Kyle living five minutes away, they suddenly had more and more time to themselves and weren't quite sure what to do with it. Mandy and Kyle stopped all the time and Tommy called as often as he could from boot camp, but, it just wasn't the same.

No more fighting the boys to get up and get ready for school. No more last minute shopping trips with Mandy as she returns from school with nothing to do for the evening. The silence was almost deafening in that house.

Ted didn't notice it as much as Elaine because he worked and saw Kyle constantly. They did manage to go out in the evenings more now. They took in an occasional movie, frequent dinners out, and he even started to like to take little shopping trips with his wife.

Something he never could see himself doing before now. He had never been big on shopping and thought of those malls chilled him to the bone. Ted just kind of lost track of Elaine having nothing but time on her hands during the day now and nothing much to do in the evening either.

They talked about her finding a part time job just to occupy her free time. But, she wasn't really sure she wanted a real job. She had always been a mom and wife and always had a houseful of kids and their friends to keep her busy.

Time seemed to be a rare commodity then. Now, she had nothing but time on her hands and it was driving her mad. Maybe a part time job was something she should at least consider she found herself thinking.

She and Ted talked about what kind of job she could get with no type of formal training. Ted suggested that he ask where he worked to see if they needed anyone on a part time basis. "What could I do where you work?" she quickly asked.

Of course he told her not to sell herself short as she was better than most men on his crew and he would be more than happy to have her work for him. She of course passed it off as pity and told him she would rather find some other type of work than construction.

He suggested she look in the want ads in the local newspaper and might even look for help wanted signs in windows where she shops. People are always looking for good dependable people he told her. She reluctantly decided that a part time job would not be the worst thing she had ever done on this earth and set about finding something.

It would help take some free time off her hands and had an added plus. She would be bringing in some extra money that might come in handy for a get away or something. Maybe this had more pluses than minuses she decided after giving it some serious thought.

Before everyone knew it she found a job in a local craft store and just loved it. She liked working with people and was great with her hands so the job seemed to be a perfect fit. They quickly found that she was an excellent salesperson as well.

She had all her friends coming in and was always selling them a new project or two. They just loved her at the store and the customers thought she was the greatest. This is something that Ted had known for years though.

Soon her days were full and her time consumed. Ted was busier than ever at work as new houses were springing up everywhere. Kyle was stepping up the ladder at work as well. They gave him his own crew and he was a natural.

Mandy was doing well in her job. She loved kids and loved teaching. Even Tommy was happy and doing what he loved and wanted. He was following his dream and it seemed that even though they weren't under the same roof, they were just as happy as ever and would be forever.

Chapter 6

Elaine was deep in thought and knee deep in a project at work when the phone rang. Her boss quickly answered not wanting to disrupt her and her train of thought. "Elaine, phone" was shouted to the back of the store. "Tell whoever it is that I'll call them back in a bit, I want to finish this" she hollered back.

Besides, she thought it was only Ted wanting to ask her out on another of the many "dates" they had been going on lately and she really didn't want to stop what she was doing. She loved their dates and the thought of spending time together but she was busy and didn't want to stop just now.

"You better take this Elaine, it's the hospital" her boss softly said as she approached her with the phone. "The hospital, now what" she said as she reached for the phone. She fully expected to hear that either Ted or Kyle was in for stitches and needed a ride home. She really wasn't prepared nor expecting the news she received instead.

"Elaine, this is doctor Blake, I have Ted in here and you better get down here as soon as you can" the voice on the other end said. "I'll be right there" was all she could muster as her mind was racing with the worst of thoughts.

Her boss understood and even offered to close the store and drive her if she wanted her to. She said she would be fine and that it was probably just stitches. "They are the biggest babies when they are hurt" she said. Not knowing if she was trying to convince her boss or herself.

They both kind of laughed and Elaine was off to see just what had happened. The doctor really never said just what had happened. Just that he had Ted there and she could come down. Probably another set of stitches and he doesn't want Ted driving, she thought as she neared the hospital driveway.

She entered the emergency entrance and immediately saw Kyle and several of the men from Ted's crew in the waiting room. Her heart nearly stopped when she saw the look on her sons face. "What is it Kyle?" she asked her son over and over. Her son was white as a sheet and told his mom to sit down and he would tell her what had happened.

He had just begun to tell his mom what had happened when Mandy came in and asked what had happened as well. Kyle told them both to sit down and he would explain it to them together. He saw no sense in telling the story twice. Besides, he had enough difficulty telling it once.

They sat there holding hands and fearing the worst, specially with all the men from work there. Each and every one of them had a look she had never seen before on their hardened sun tanned faces. She and Mandy both knew this was no joke. Kyle told them that a terrible accident had happened and he was to blame. "If anything happens to dad, it's my fault" he told his mom and sister, then broke down.

One of the men from their crew walked over, put his hand on Kyle's shoulder, and told them not to listen to a word he says. "Kyle is just worked up like we all are and worried about Ted" the man told them. He assured Elaine that Kyle had nothing to do with the accident and should stop blaming himself for it.

The man told them that it was no ones fault and no one was to blame. If anything, he assured them, it would be faulty equipment that was to blame. He told them that they were putting a steel beam into place and Ted was close enough to hear the cable snap.

The beam would have crushed Kyle had Ted not dove and pushed him out of harms way. "If it wasn't for Ted, Kyle might not be standing here right now" he told them. "Ted is a hero and saved Kyle's life" the man went on.

Just then the doctor appeared and told Elaine that he needed to speak to her and the family, immediately. She and the kids both feared the worst but followed him into a nearby conference room. They sat together and just hugged and comforted each other bracing for what they all knew was certain to be devastating news.

"Ted is alive and is going to remain that way" he started. "I want you all to put those fears out of your mind once and for all" he went on. "But, there is a very serious problem, we just aren't sure yet how serious it is or will be" the doctor went on to say.

"It seems that when Ted dove to push Kyle out of the way, the beam landed across his legs pinning him to the ground." "It appears that right now we are faced with both knees being crushed" the doctor said. "We just aren't sure how serious this will be down the road until he wakes up and can stand to be without the pain medication we have him on right now."

"We have him on some very serious pain medicine right now and will have for the next few days" their doctor told them. "Right now he needs to rest and not move around." "The only way we can assure this is to keep him sedated and calm" he said.

He went on to explain that Ted wouldn't really even be aware that they were there until he stabilized and could go without the rather potent medication he was on. "At that point we can take a look at the damage and give a more decisive prognosis" he said.

"Until then, we are just guessing and we don't want to do that" he told Elaine. "We want to be certain Elaine, I'm sure you want us to be as well" he said. She assured him she wanted only what was best for Ted and asked if they could see him now. "You all can go in and see him but he won't know that you're there" he said.

He showed them to Ted's room and told Elaine that he would go out and tell the guys the news so they weren't left in the dark. She hadn't even thought about that but said she would appreciate it if he could take care of that for them. "Right now I'll just leave you all with this" he went on to say.

"Ted is alive, I believe at this point the worst we are looking at is him being off his feet for a while and needing as much help as he can get." "I will know more and we can go into more detail when he wakes up and can go without the meds" he finished.

As he walked away Elaine and both of her children vowed to do anything they could to help him. Elaine knew that they would be there to help her with anything he or she might need and that was a huge load off her at that point. She also knew his company thought the world of him and would do whatever was needed to help in any way they could as well.

She just knew that they wouldn't turn their back on him at a time like this. She also knew most of the men in his and Kyle's crews and knew they would move heaven and earth to help her and Ted both if they needed it. Those men loved and respected Ted and would do anything they could for him, she just knew it.

They slowly opened the door and peered in to see him sleeping peacefully. They all drew a collective sigh of relief and Kyle dropped to his knees at his dads beside and lost it. He sobbed uncontrollably and still blamed himself for this happening. His mom and sister both stood beside him and said they knew this wasn't his fault and told him to stop blaming himself.

"Your dad would kick your tail for acting like this and you know it" his mom said. "I know mom" he said as he squeezed his dad's hand and sat beside his bed. "Let's all pull together and help each other so we can get him and us all through this" Elaine told her children.

They both knew she was right and pulled themselves together and just sat there watching the man they had always thought was invincible, laying there motionless. It hurt them to think that he didn't know they were there for him when he needed them the most. Or so they thought.

It was at that point Ted somehow miraculously patted his son on the head and asked "where am I?" They all nearly fainted. Kyle couldn't believe his dad had just woke up but was glad he had. It put most of his worst fears to rest, for the time being anyway.

Elaine bent down and softly told him that a hospital was a heck of a way to get a vacation. He softly smiled and told her that he would take one any way he could get one. Mandy rushed out to get the doctor and tell him her dad was somehow awake.

He was astonished when she told him. "There is no way he should be awake, let alone speaking or making any sense" the doctor told her. "Well, you know my dad" she said as he followed her to the room.

Sure enough as he entered the room, he heard Ted carrying on a somewhat intelligent conversation with his wife and son.

"Well I'll be" he said as he went to Ted's bedside. "You shouldn't even be awake big guy" he told Ted. "I gave you enough pain medicine to drop a rhinoceros" he went on. Ted simply told him that maybe he was tougher than a rhino and softly smirked.

"Well, since you are awake, I'll fill you in on what is going on too" he said. The doctor told him that his legs had been hurt when the beam fell and right now they weren't sure of the extent until he had a chance to rest and get stronger. "So lay there and be a good boy while I try and keep you still and asleep" he said.

Asking if Ted was in any pain before he left he told them not to wear him out any more than he already was. "He really does need his rest" he told them as he closed the door. Elaine knew the doctor was right but she wasn't about to leave him like this. She just couldn't bring herself to walk out and leave him all alone.

After some prodding from Kyle and Mandy, she did agree to go to the cafeteria with them and at the very least, get something to eat. "It won't do dad or you any good to not eat mom" Mandy told her. She knew her daughter was right and Ted had already dropped back into a drug induced sleep, so this would be the perfect time to step out for a while. Even if it was for a very short while.

Sitting at the table waiting for her children to return with their food she dropped her head into her hands and let the tears flow. She had never thought about anything like this happening to Ted before and now she wasn't sure how to handle it or what to do for him.

It was strange and unfamiliar territory for all of them. He had always been their rock and they all just never thought about him being seriously ill or hurt like this before. Mandy returned first and just knelt down and hugged her mom. "Let it go mom" she said as she held her mother close.

After what one might call dinner and some small talk, they decided that they somehow had to get in touch with Tommy. At the very least, they needed to let him know what was going on. "He would want to know" Elaine told her children. Kyle agreed that he should be told and told his mom that he would somehow get word to him.

"I'll run over to the recruiters office, they'll know how to get word to him" Kyle told his mom as he gathered his things. "Thank you Kyle" was all she could manage. He hugged and kissed his mother softly on the cheek and told her to call his cell if anything happened or she needed anything. She said she would and thanked him again before he left.

"Just tell Tommy we don't need him leaving boot camp for this as we really don't know if it is serious or not at this point" she said to her son. "He doesn't need to do anything as drastic as that" she went on. Kyle told her that somehow he would speak to Tommy personally and let him know what had happened and that there was no reason to rush home right now.

He quickly left to see how to contact his brother and at least let him know what was going on. He knew his mom was right, Tommy adored dad and would want to know if he was hurt. The recruiter's office seemed like the only logical place to start, so off he went.

Elaine and Mandy went back to Ted's room to find him sleeping comfortably and in no apparent pain or discomfort. They both decided this might be a good time to slip out for the evening and go home. Mandy knew her mom would stay all night if she let her, and she wasn't about to let her.

"I'll go home with you mom and we can start making calls" she said. Elaine knew her daughter was right again. They needed to let friends and family know what had happened before they heard it from someone else and got the details all blown out of proportion. She didn't want to start getting sympathy calls about his untimely demise.

Elaine and Mandy both went to his side, bent down and kissed him softly on the cheek and told him goodnight. He didn't even stir so they knew the drugs had finally taken hold and he would be out the rest of the night. Elaine whispered I love you in his ear before gathering her things and following her daughter to the parking lot.

Mandy told her mom that she would follow her home and they

would make all the necessary calls there. Elaine could only shake her head yes and got into her car. As she fastened her seat belt and started the car, she once again let the tears flow. She somehow felt guilty leaving him alone like this.

They pulled into the drive and immediately saw several vehicles and people gathered at their house. Somehow friends and a few family members had already gotten word and were there waiting to see if they could help in any way.

She could only smile and think that this is exactly why Ted wanted to stay here in Council Bluffs, the people. They would drop everything to help and wouldn't take no, or I'm fine for an answer. They genuinely cared for one of their own and would do anything for you. She quickly opened the front door and went to start a pot of coffee.

Mandy met people at the door and took jackets and things and helped her mom and several friends in the kitchen. Soon they were all gathered in the living room and Elaine told them what had happened and the condition Ted was in. They were genuinely concerned and assured her that she needn't worry about anything. They were there to help.

Family, friends and neighbors all offered help in any way she could imagine. From watching the house, preparing meals, taking care of the lawn to monetary help if they needed it. They all stepped up and promised that she wouldn't have to worry about a thing. They would all take care of everything. And she knew they meant it.

It felt good to have friends, family and a community care for you and your family like that. She too thought that this must be one of the reasons her and Ted never moved away. The people were absolutely wonderful and they were genuine. They didn't offer just to save face within the community or to make themselves look good with a personal agenda. They really wanted to help.

She told them that she and Ted both appreciated all the heartfelt help and that she may indeed take most of them up on their offers. She knew that for a short time at the very least, she would be spending a lot of time at the hospital and could use the help. As her and Mandy personally thanked and shook hands with everyone, Kyle came in.

He told his mom that he had been in touch with Tommy. He told her that he promised Tommy that if anything serious happened, he would call and let him know so he could make arrangements to come home. Tommy although wracked with concern for his dad, had agreed to stay where he was and continue his training.

He also made it very clear that should something serious come of this. He would be on the first plane home. Elaine was just happy that her son had been level headed enough to stay until they knew just what was going to happen next. And right now, that was something that none of them knew.

Chapter 7

    The next several days were a blur and full of confusion and uncertainty to say the least. Ted was in and out of consciousness from the pain medication they had him on. At times it seemed that he was coherent and alert and other times he made absolutely no sense at all. Everyone knew that it was the effect of the drugs and they had to be as patient as they could until he was able to be off them.

    Elaine knew that the pain had to be excruciating and could only watch and wait. That was the hardest part for everyone, waiting. Men from his crew stopped by nightly and just sat by his bed hoping for one of the scarce times he was alert enough to talk.

    Doctor Blake was remarkable at keeping them in the loop every step of the way through this very rough and uncertain time. He gave them constant updates. At times he acted like Ted was the only patient he had and gave him his full and undivided attention.

    They all knew he was a very busy man but appreciated him giving Ted the attention he did. They knew that Ted was in good hands and trusted him fully. Days came and went without much change or reason for hope or expectations of good news.

    After several weeks Ted was able to go without the high doses of pain medicine they had been giving him and was now alert and in good spirits most of the time. Nights seemed to be the worst and still found him needing the medication in higher doses.

    He was finally able to withstand the tests and examinations the doctor had to put him through to determine the extent of his injuries and the damage if any. Only after a full battery of tests, x-rays, MRI's and examinations, was doctor Blake ready to sit down with them and give his diagnosis.

    Ted and Elaine had already spoken and had some idea of things that would need to be done and weren't completely taken by surprise when the doctor finally gave them the news. As they had expected, Ted would have to undergo surgery on both knees to reconstruct them. They both had been crushed by the beam and needed to be

For Better, For Worse?

done as soon as possible to deter any type of permanent damage.

They were also prepared for what he said next and fully expected it. Doctor Blake confirmed their suspicions that he would have to go through some very intense and long physical therapy after surgery and a recovery period. Again, this they expected.

The doctor went on to say that he would give them some time to discuss this as it would be a major surgery. He also told them that although a major surgery, it was routine as well and done daily. He told them to consult another doctor for a second opinion should they want to. But, told them he only consulted with the best specialists in the area on this matter and he had full confidence in their findings.

He told them that he only consulted with people he would trust his family or his own health with and would have no reservations in allowing them to perform this work. He told them he just gave them a lot to think about and said he would check back on them later and closed the door so they could have some privacy.

This was not something they were unprepared for. They had gone over every possible scenario in their minds and discussed every option and possibility. Elaine knew that if there was any chance for Ted to walk again and feel whole, he would have to have the surgery.

Ted too knew that surgery would be his only option because the only other option would be to do nothing and never walk again. That was not about to happen he had told Elaine. "I have a little girl to walk down an aisle someday soon and I'm not going to do that from a wheelchair."

She knew in her heart that his mind was made up and she knew that she fully agreed with his decision. She too wanted him to at least have every chance and option available to him to walk and be normal again. Not for her sake, she would take care of him whether he could walk or not, but for his.

She knew her husband and knew that he would do whatever it took to get back to where he was before this happened. That was one of the many things she loved about this man, his undying determination. He took her hand in his, kissed her deeply and simply said, "let's do this."

She knew this was the right choice and would not second guess or doubt it. She asked if he wanted her to go find the doctor and he simply smiled and nodded his head yes. She quickly found the doctor and arrangements were made for his surgery.

They both thought the sooner the better and saw no reason to put it off or prolong this. Doctor Blake said he would make all the arrangements and was sure they could schedule him in a day or two. He told them in the mean time, just enjoy each other.

His surgery was set in two days and his room was constantly full of friends, family, his children and co-workers. Everyone stopped by and his room looked like the distribution center for a florist.

Flowers were everywhere, balloons, cards, stuffed animals and the guys from his crew even brought him a do it yourself birdhouse kit to put together. They told him even they had confidence that he could handle a glue bottle and complete this project.

His eyes were bright and had that spark in them that she loved so much. His color had returned and he looked good. He laughed and joked with them all and she just knew that he was going into this with the best attitude anyone could have. He seemed to have no fear.

Of course the day of his surgery, the waiting room was full to overflowing with family, friends and people he worked with. Everyone paced and watched the door. Every time the door would open they all jumped and looked with anticipation for some kind of word on how Ted was doing.

They were all on pins and needles yet tried to have an upbeat and positive attitude at the same time. It almost looked like half the town had turned out to support them. Time seemed to drag on forever and patience was beginning to wear thin. Just then the doctor appeared, saw the mob and only gave a thumbs up sign.

He took Elaine, Kyle and Mandy into a nearby conference room and told them the surgery had gone smoothly and nothing unexpected was experienced or found. He told them only time will tell now and the physical therapy would help immensely. He did tell them that they found some nerve damage but fully expected that.

At the worst, they all believed he might have a slight limp and susceptible to the cold. He said they expected a full recovery and said he would be back in his room in a few hours. He told them that the anesthesia they used would keep him asleep most of the day, so they could go eat or something to pass the time.

As they emerged from the room, they were immediately surrounded by concerned friends and family. Elaine assured everyone that the surgery had gone smoothly and he would be out most of the day from the medication they gave him. The crowd erupted with cheers and well wishes for Ted and all of them.

This time she had no qualms about going home to rest and make something to eat for her and the kids. As a matter of fact, she was so excited that she invited everyone over for something to eat and to just relax for a while. She knew in her heart it was something each and every one of them could use right now.

Soon the house and yard were full of friends, family and neighbors preparing the grill and making food for everyone. This was time she could use right now. Away from nurses, doctors and that hospital food. She also knew that Ted would be in and out of sleep and right now, rest was what he needed more than visitors.

She had left her number with the nurse if they needed to get in touch with her. She felt more at ease today than she had in weeks. It was good to just sit and relax with her children and family and not worry about anything for a few hours.

Dusk was quickly approaching and she wanted to go back to the hospital just in case Ted did wake up. She didn't want him waking up to find no one there and being concerned or confused. She was just glad this part of this new journey was behind them now and the doctors didn't think he would have any type of complications.

She knew her husband and he could live with a slight limp and some uneasiness when the cold weather approached. He was one of the toughest men she knew and just knew that something this minor wouldn't slow him down a bit.

She entered his room to find him sitting up and the nurse giving him some ice chips and 7-Up to drink. Elaine soon discovered that he had been awake for a short time and had been able to keep some saltine crackers down as well. Elaine was elated that he was awake and hungry. "Good to see you have some sort of appetite" she said as she walked over and gave her husband a kiss.

He surprised her by swatting her on the bottom. "Good to see you're a bit frisky as well" she said as she hugged him and rubbed her butt. As he cleared the cobwebs from his somewhat fuzzy mind, he asked how it went. She told him the doctors think at worst he might have a slight limp but nothing serious.

They sat and talked about his recovery and how much longer he might be in the hospital. Although they really hadn't thought about asking the doctor about this, they figured that another couple of weeks would be a safe bet. The nurse overheard them and simply shook her head yes to Elaine.

They both knew that he would want to monitor him constantly and work with him in therapy before letting him go home. Ted told her that his butt was starting to hurt from laying in that bed but he knew that right now there was nothing they could do about it. They both were quite certain that the doctor's orders forbid any type of activity or getting out of bed just yet.

The rest of the evening was spent just sitting together, holding hands, watching television and small talk. Kyle and Mandy stopped for a while and they all had a few laughs when Ted asked if either of them wanted to race. It did them all good to see him in such good spirits.

Silence fell in the room as they watched TV and soon they all noticed that he was fast asleep once more. Deciding it better to not wake him, they one by one kissed his cheek, told him they loved him and slipped out without a sound. Outside they all said their goodbye's and I love you's before each headed off in their own direction for their respective homes.

Chapter 8

Just as they expected Ted was kept in the hospital and started working with physical therapists daily to get him ready to return home. Actually he was kept for several weeks and when the day came for him to go home, he was more than ready. He was discharged only after he and Elaine both agreed to follow the doctor's orders to the letter.

Those orders included his use of a wheelchair anywhere outside his home. Inside the home he could use two canes they sent home with him or a walker. He was not to return to work in any capacity and was told they didn't know just exactly when he would be allowed to. He agreed to be a good boy and follow the doctor's orders. Elaine of course assured Dr. Blake that he would, or else.

That was probably the hardest part of all this on Ted. Elaine knew that he would want to get back to work as soon as he could. The company had been great and their work comp. insurance carrier never bickered when it came to paying him his benefits or paying the medical bills. They had stepped up and did the right thing and she was thankful they had.

The company had stood up for him and told their insurance carrier that if they even thought about fighting him on this, they would be his best witnesses. As a matter of fact, they had even caught the accident on video tape. The crane operator had a cameraman with him so they could use the footage for advertising.

A copy of the tape was given to Elaine right after the incident just in case she needed to obtain an attorney and fight this. She was glad they had done it but vowed to never show the tape to Ted unless it was necessary in a court battle. Him living the accident over and over was something that she really didn't think he needed.

Kyle, Mandy and even Tommy agreed that the only time he should be shown the tape is if it was needed in court. If it wasn't, they saw no reason for him to ever know it existed. With everyone in agreement, she quickly put the tape in their safe deposit box at the bank and decided to forget it was there.

Of course a huge party was planned for his return home. All of his co-workers and owners of the company and their families were there. Friends, family and neighbors were all there and the city even gave them permission to close off the street in front of their house for it. It was a huge success and Ted was the life of the party.

The guys from work even took turns pushing him up and down the street in his wheelchair and Kyle was the time keeper. It was quite a sight to see Elaine thought. She was just glad to have him home, the rest would work itself out as they went along. Ted was the last to give up and call it a night, having to say goodbye and make sure everyone got off safely.

She couldn't get over it, he was the one that was hurt and he still acted like the mother hen. Making sure everyone got home safely. She was glad to see the old Ted back and glad she wouldn't be sleeping alone for another night. She had missed him terribly and couldn't wait to feel him next to her tonight.

She did have a little fear though of rolling or tossing in her sleep and hurting his knees. She even thought about letting him have the bed and she would sleep on the couch until he was better healed. He wouldn't hear of it and told her she would sleep with him just like she had every night for all these years.

She was glad he felt that way but just knew she wouldn't sleep a wink all night. As they got ready for bed she made sure he took his pain medication and helped him to bed. Only after he was settled and comfortable did she even attempt to get in with him.

She was glad that they had a king size bed that gave him plenty of room. She propped up his legs and iced them down before turning in for the night herself. He pulled her to him, cradled her in his arms and soon was sound asleep.

Having him home was a process she had to get used to. Walker, canes, wheelchair, medicine, it was mind numbing at times but she weathered it like a trooper. She drove him to physical therapy every day and watched him struggle. He was constantly pushing himself to do more than he knew he was capable of.

His therapists were constantly telling him to slow down and take it easy. He was never one to take it easy though she thought. She knew her husband and knew he would do whatever it took to overcome this and come back stronger than ever. Ted was after all, Ted.

After nearly a month of intense therapy Ted just knew that something wasn't right. He wasn't able to do most of the things he was able to do before the accident and it was starting to concern him. Of course the doctors ran more tests and took countless x-rays to make sure something hadn't happened internally to re-injure his knees.

They found nothing out of the ordinary but started to re-evaluate just what degree of recovery he might attain after all. They were starting to fear the damage was worse than they originally thought and he might have a permanent injury that would restrict him from ever returning to work at all.

This was something he didn't want to hear, nor was he ready to sit around home feeling sorry for himself and just give up. He was torn inside with all the uncertainty and knew there was nothing they could do but keep hope alive. That job was his life and he just couldn't bear to think that it might be something he would have to consider giving up all together.

He could only hope the company would find a position for him that would still keep him active within the company without the physical portion he was so used to. They had been great so far and always said they would do whatever it took to have him back at work. He could only hope they meant what they said.

After another two months of therapy and doctors running test after test it became clear that his knees had healed as well as they ever would. He still had trouble standing for any amount of time and walking was difficult at times as well. He was starting to resign himself to the idea that the doctors might be right. Maybe he wouldn't be able to return to work after all.

The owners of the company of course said that they would make sure he was treated right and fairly should it come to that. But, they also told him that they could not let him come back in any capacity unless the doctors gave him a clean bill of health and a full and unconditional return to work slip. He was quite certain that wasn't going to happen though.

He was a little confused to the stance they seemed to be taking now. They had assured him they would do whatever it took to get him back to work. Why now did they seem to say they couldn't accommodate him without that "unconditional" return to work slip? He later found out that their insurance carrier was the one that pushed that issue and would not budge on their position.

All he could do now was wait and see what the final word from the doctors would be then plan some sort of life from there. If he couldn't return to work, he just knew that Elaine would have to find a full time job to help out with the bills.

He decided he could get rid of some things and pay off as much as he could but knew in his heart that she would need to find work in order to keep them afloat financially. That killed him inside to even think such a thing as she had never had to work in all the years they had been together.

He wasn't even sure at this point if she could find a job that would pay enough to make it worth her time. After all, she really didn't have any sort of skills outside the home. And other than the craft store, had never held a job of any kind.

He knew that the insurance company would have to make a settlement of some kind with him but was very sure it wouldn't be enough to pay everything off. Even through all the uncertainty and pain, he never doubted his actions and if the same situation arose, he would do it all over again.

Even if the person he was saving wasn't his son. He knew deep inside himself that he had made the right decision and would do it all over again if he had to. He wasn't about to sit and blame anyone or anything for what had happened. He just accepted it as fate or the will of God and left it at that.

He also knew that all the worry and second guessing in the world wouldn't do him any good until the doctors were completely sure of what was going to happen and when. There was no sense in trying to brace himself for the worst if all he needed was more time to heal and recover. It really hadn't been that much time yet and he had been through a serious injury and surgery.

He had seen it before, one person gets hurt and bounces back in a few days. Another person has the same injury and takes several weeks or months to recover fully. Maybe he was just a slow healer and would take a little more time than some. Maybe he was working himself up over nothing after all.

He decided not to worry Elaine with all this until it was certain that they really needed to sit down and look at this realistically. He also decided to follow the doctors and therapists orders to the letter and would slow down and quit pushing himself so hard.

That might be the only thing that is wrong too he thought. He knew he had been pushing harder than he should to get back to normal. Maybe he was just pushing too hard too fast. He promised himself to take it easier and to listen fully to the doctors.

Elaine suddenly noticed a day and night change in him. He was following the doctor and therapists orders completely. If they told him to slow down, he did. He didn't argue or push it, he just did as he was told. He used his walker and canes faithfully and was the model patient from then on.

She didn't know what had gotten into him but she was sure glad for whatever it was. He took his medicine and even went in for extra whirlpool baths to relax and soothe his knees. He was the patient that all doctors dream of having and was on his best behavior. She was so proud of him and glad he decided not to fight it or push it any longer.

If he was going to be one hundred percent again, it would be because he did as instructed. He wouldn't be able to look back and say "if only I had listened." He took his meds and iced down his knees faithfully. Something she and Kyle usually had to try and strap him down to do. Now he asked for it and never complained.

She was sure this all would work and before he realized it, he would be back to his old self barking out orders on a construction site. That was something they both agreed they could never lose sight of, hope. They both agreed that no matter what happened next, they would get through it together. They had been through rough times before and would get through this just fine.

Ted had to believe deep inside himself that with a little more time and work, he would be back at work and his old self again. He knew in his heart that Elaine and the kids would stick by him no matter what. He also knew that he would never feel whole again unless he knew in his heart that he had given it his all. He had all the faith in the world and support of friends and family that would get him through this.

Chapter 9

After another month of intense and vigorous physical therapy and following the doctors order to the letter, the news he was dreading came. The damage was more severe than originally thought and Ted would not in fact be able to return to work. He was devastated yet expecting it at the same time.

This wasn't something out of the blue as Ted and Elaine had both sat and talked about this very possibility. They had discussed the possible need for her to find a job just in case the insurance settlement fell short of paying all the bills.

He immediately told Elaine that he would sell off all his tools and anything else he felt no longer needed to make their debt load less. She of course wouldn't hear of it and assured him they would be fine. She told him that if she needed to find a job she would do exactly that and between his disability and her check the bills would be paid. He was so very proud of her for taking it like this. He had fully expected her to fight him every step of the way on it.

The next logical step was to approach his job with the news that he would be unable to ever return. The owners were crushed that they were losing the best employee they had ever had. Ted was one of the very first people they had hired after starting the company.

He had been with them stride for stride in all their growth and successes. They weren't excited about him not being there to help shape and grow the company into the future. But, they fully understood and in a way, had expected this. They had always been a bit unsure if he would fully recover and be allowed to come back to work.

They did as they said they would do though and fought beside him all the way to assure a proper and fair settlement from the insurance company. He was thankful of that, almost expecting them to write him off and fight him instead. Of course, from what he had known of them from the start, they just weren't that type of people.

They stood beside him, helped him get every penny owed him and even said he was welcome to stop by anytime he wanted. It would just have to be in the capacity of a visitor and not an employee.

It nearly killed him inside to clean out his belongings and say his final farewells to his crew and friends. Everyone on the site was in tears that day, even the owners. Ted knew that this was just the end of a chapter in his life and the beginning of a new one.

He wasn't sure where it would lead them or what they would encounter along the way. He only knew that he and Elaine would make the trip together. They would somehow get through this and everything would be fine. He had to believe that right now. He just had to.

The settlement from the insurance company was a fair one after all. His old boss had made sure of that. What Ted didn't know was his old boss had reminded the insurance company of the existence of that tape. And, he made darn sure the insurance people knew that Elaine had a copy.

It saddened them to see their friends have to go through this and they weren't about to let the insurance people screw them over now. The insurance adjustor even suggested to Ted's old boss that his little threat might be construed as blackmail. His old boss just laughed and said, "so sue me."

After Ted's departure, Kyle stepped up and took on more responsibility and stepped right into his dads shoes. Ted couldn't be prouder of his son for stepping up like that and showing his old company that they hadn't lost him after all. They just gained a younger version of him.

Kyle was a natural and he and Elaine was so very proud of him for doing it. It wasn't long before his old crew was stopping by to keep him up to date on all the goings on. It was at times like he had never left at all. They all stayed in touch and continued to do so even after he and Elaine's breakup.

As soon as the settlement check was deposited and all the bills they could pay were paid, they sat back and took a look at just where they were financially. It was soon apparent that Elaine would in fact have to find a full time job if they were going to make it. She had been secretly applying for jobs since the news that Ted wouldn't be allowed to go back to work had been received. Shortly before Ted's disability payments started, she was offered a full time position at a local warehouse pulling parts for a local auto parts chain.

She would pull parts and pack them into totes to be sent to various store locations the company owned. After she filled the orders, she would take them to the shipping department to be distributed to the stores.

Ted soon found that she was being paid a very decent wage and the work was neither hard nor demanding. The company also offered some very attractive benefits that most smaller companies don't usually offer. He thought her lucky to have found such a job.

The hours were even appealing to her. She started early in the morning and was off by early afternoon. This still gave her time to do any shopping that Ted couldn't do or help him with things around home that needed to be done. She got to spend a lot of time with him and still work a full time job, receiving a decent paycheck every week.

It was the best of all worlds and she was happy that she was finally helping. She had never told Ted this, but, she had always felt that she never did enough to help before he was hurt. Ted always worked and brought home the money and she just helped spend it.

She had never really felt that she was pulling her fair share of the load and always kind of wanted to. She was just afraid that he would have dismissed the idea and told her that he would make the money and for her to just spend it.

Now most women would have been elated but Elaine always wanted to help. Now she was getting to and it pleased her very much. Besides, it wasn't like Ted was just sitting at home with no income of any kind. She wasn't supporting a lazy and worthless man like so many women do these days. He had his disability check coming in and assumed as much of the housework as he could physically do.

He still had trouble standing for any long periods and walking was still a little difficult at times as well. They both knew that with time his stamina and endurance would improve and he would find walking easier and standing not so difficult. It was going to just take time and time was something that he now found he had an abundance of. He still faithfully did his exercises the therapist had taught him and walked as much and as often as he could. Slowly he was getting better, just never better enough to go back to work.

Time actually passed quickly and soon Ted was as good as he would ever be. He was able to stand for longer periods and was walking with just the slightest of limps. He still couldn't walk great distances but could last long enough for shopping outings or grocery store visits with Elaine. Her job was coming along nicely and before she knew it she had gotten a raise and the two went out to dinner to celebrate her new success.

Before they knew it, Mandy was busy making wedding preparations and he would soon have one of the most important walks of his life. Walking his little girl down the aisle to give her away. He always joked about how good it sounded to "give her away" but now that the time was near, he couldn't be sadder.

He was elated and joyed that she had found that one person she just knew she wanted to spend her life with. It was the giving away part that her dad wasn't overly thrilled with. He knew that Dan was a good man and thought the world of him. He just wasn't looking forward to the giving away thing.

The wedding day was upon them and Ted not only walked his daughter down that aisle, but got the first dance with her as well. Tommy made it back for his sisters wedding and looked so handsome and grown up in his uniform.

He was now stationed at a permanent duty station and was considering applying for a spot as instructor at one of the Navy's schools. He was doing so very well and he and his long time girlfriend Debbie, were discussing wedding bells as well. The family was growing and before they knew it, there would be grandchildren.

This was something neither of them really looked forward to.

Only because it would signify the fact that they were getting older. They would welcome grandchildren with open arms and all the love in the universe. They had always secretly talked between themselves at how thrilled they would be to become grandparents.

They just wouldn't embrace the thought of getting older just yet. Even though at times, Ted's knees made him feel like he was ninety instead of his late forties. Of course Elaine only counted a half year older for every birthday so she was only in her twenties. According to her anyway.

Before they knew it, bills were caught up and they even had a small amount of money in savings again. It was all due to Elaine and her new job and Ted gave her all the credit she deserved. She was proud of herself and of Ted. He had fought back to a point where he could feel comfortable with himself and the way his injury had ended.

He was finally recovered and on his way to doing more and more. He was almost back to the old Ted she knew and loved and things were all in all good again. They enjoyed their time alone and made the most of it most of the time.

In the back of her mind Elaine just couldn't shake the feeling that somehow they had lost something over these very trying and exhausting months since Ted's injury. She felt as though a wedge had been driven between them and didn't quite know what to do about it.

She knew that Ted was living in his own hell from what had happened. And, she knew that it was something that she just couldn't grasp. After all, she hadn't experienced it first hand and wasn't sure how she would handle it had the tables been turned.

She was sure that she would have been unable to handle things as well as Ted had. Nonetheless, she still felt a growing distance and that scared her immensely. For the first time in her marriage to this wonderful, caring man, she felt like she was at times living with a stranger. He would snap at her and tell her that he was dealing with all this the best he could.

It wasn't that she doubted him, she just didn't know how to help him and that hurt her deeply. He had always been the one they depended on to support them and keep the family running smoothly. Now he had to lean on her and depend on her to support him and that was a position he was not accustomed to.

Nor was it one he welcomed becoming accustomed to. It killed him inside to know that she had to work. They both seemed to handle all this the best they could but she was starting to feel like she needed something more.

Time also brought some unwanted and unexpected changes to them. Elaine seemed to go out more by herself, visiting friends from work he had never met. She seemed to be taking on a life of her own and it included him less and less. She seemed more distant as time went by. He couldn't put his finger on it but had some very unpleasant suspicions.

He had driven her away a bit during his struggle to overcome his injury. At times he even caught himself being a little cold and distant to her. She would always try, but he just couldn't let her in. He recalls telling her "you can't know how I feel because you have never been through anything like this before."

That was wrong on his part, very wrong. He snapped at her only because he felt sorry for himself and the fact that he might not be one hundred percent again, ever. That wasn't her fault but he couldn't help himself from being a bit cold and defensive at times.

He knew that if she was becoming distant now, it was because he had made her that way. And, he knew that he had only one person to blame, himself. He was more determined than ever to make things work between them and was the first to tell her so.

She just dismissed it as her being tired from work and assured him that everything was fine. He knew in his heart that things weren't fine but for the time being, was content to believe her. A year passed since his accident and he suddenly found them both distancing themselves from each other even more.

It seemed the more she went out with friends the more suspicious he became and that only drives them even further apart. Instead of sitting and talking about things like old times, they now screamed and fought. He couldn't swear to it, but it seemed that more and more Elaine would purposely start an argument just to keep her distance from him.

The one thing he was sure of was things were definitely getting worse between them. No matter what he tried, nothing seemed to work. She just pushed harder away from him and he knew that something was terribly wrong.

The more distance she seemed to put between them the more he tried to pull them back together. It was a constant battle anymore and he just couldn't imagine things getting any worse. But they would get much worse.

Chapter 10

___They say time heals all wounds but in their case time only seemed to make things worse and drive them further and further apart. Of course they concealed it well from friends and family. If one would see them together, they would swear the old Ted and Elaine were stronger than ever. They put on a brave front for all they knew and Ted fully intended to keep doing it. Even the kids had no idea their parents were having problems of any kind.

Ted's suspicions of her cheating were fast approaching obsession. In his mind he just knew that she had turned to someone new. It had to be another man and he decided to find out for himself once and for all. Every time he confronted her she just brushed him off and told him he was worrying about nothing.

He was starting to catch her in lie after lie. She would say that she was going to one of her friends from work's house and disappear. He would call her friends and ask to speak to her only to find her not there. One time her friend even volunteered the information that she had called and said she couldn't make it and said she would see her at work the next day.

That only made his mind race with possibilities he didn't want to imagine. He started checking her cell phone activity online only to find call after call to a number he had never seen before. Uncertain of how he would ever find out who the number belonged to, he decided to ask her about it.

Of course she told him it was a friend from work and told him he was making a lot out of nothing. He finally found a friend that was able to help him. He knew a woman that worked at the phone company and told her his daughter had this number on her cell phone and it was a number he didn't recognize.

She of course helped and said to keep the information quiet as she could get in trouble for helping. It was quickly discovered that the number was to a man Elaine worked with and calls had been placed and received at various times and days. They had even called each other on weekends. Mostly while he was out running errands or going for his daily walks. Now his mind really was racing.

Why had she lied to him about this? If this guy was just a friend from work, why hadn't she invited him to the house? As his detective's skills became sharper, he discovered letters she had written to someone hidden in her car.

They were love letters to someone, but who? She had been smart enough not to put anyone's name on the heading but it was plain to see that she was telling this person her innermost feelings.

Several of their friends had approached Ted and told him about seeing her with a strange man at the mall or other locations and they seemed to be very friendly. He of course covered and said it was a guy she worked with and that he had met him and his intentions were purely honorable.

It hurt him very much to lie to their friends like this but he felt that he had no choice. Her visits to friends he had never met were becoming almost constant and she seemed to be staying out later and later at night. This didn't seem to bother her even though it was apparent that it was bothering Ted.

Of course he would pretend to be asleep when she came in so she felt confident that she had pulled it off successfully. He wanted her to think that he had no idea that anything out of the ordinary was happening. He noticed on more than one instance that she came in late, put the clothes she had been wearing immediately in the washing machine and jumped into the shower. Not wanting to instigate a fight, he overlooked this and sought out professional help.

He approached a marriage counselor a friend of his referred him to and asked about all of these warning signs. He was told that one of the most telling signs of a cheating spouse was the washing of clothes and showering immediately upon returning home.

According to this expert, the washing of clothes and immediate shower is the cheaters way of washing away all evidence that they had been with someone else. Like washing away aftershave or cologne from a stranger that he would immediately know wasn't his. This is their way of washing it all away so you have no clue to their infidelity.

According to the counselor, this was more than a coincidence, it was a sign not to be ignored. He confirmed the phone calls, letters and disappearances where all unmistakable signs that she was cheating. He knew in his heart that it was all true but just couldn't bring himself to accept it or confront her on it.

He left things as they were for a couple of months to build her confidence that she was succeeding with her little "fling." It worked beautifully and soon she was confident that Ted had no idea what she was doing and started to become a bit sloppy in concealing things. He began to find more revealing letters. The phone calls were almost constant now and he just knew that it was time to find out once and for all just what was going on.

He called his old boss and told him of his need to earn some extra money, fast. He said he was even willing to work at night and be paid under the table to make this money. His friend soon gave him some work he could handle without fear of further injury or re-injury.

He decided to let Ted do some work for him on side jobs that didn't go through the companies books anyway. He was able to work during the day while Elaine was at work. It was just what he needed to help keep his mind occupied during the day. And, it helped him get the money he needed together to finally catch her with proof she couldn't deny.

As soon as he had the money he needed together, without taking it out of the bank where she would surely notice it. He sprang into action. He very discreetly hired a private detective. Actually it was a police officer friend of his that worked side jobs as a private detective.

He sat and disclosed to him what he had discovered on his own and told him what the counselor had told him to watch for. His friend quickly agreed that he would suspect her of cheating as well with no more information then he had at that moment.

His friend reluctantly took Ted's money and told him he would do this for nothing if it would help. Ted assured him that he needed to pay for gas and film and things and he didn't expect his friend to pay for this out of his pocket. And, that the offer to do it for nothing was appreciated but he wasn't about to burden his friend financially either.

His friend agreed to help but told him that he could very possibly find out some things that Ted wouldn't want found out. Ted assured him that he was prepared for the worst and that he needed to know. His friend agreed and said he would call when he had some concrete evidence that Ted could use.

Part of him wanted to find out that she had nothing more than a friend she could confide in and help her through a very trying time. Another part of him just knew that he would find all his darkest fears had became reality. He feared the latter more than anyone could ever imagine. And that, scared him to death.

He continued to work the side jobs his old boss sent his way and stockpiled some extra money should the worst happen and he needs to find a place of his own, and find it quick. He honestly hoped that if confronted with proof, Elaine would come to her senses and want to work things out. He really didn't want to see their marriage of more than twenty-five years end like this.

A few weeks passed and Elaine acted like everything was back to normal. Her disappearances didn't seem to lessen, if anything, they got more frequent and lasted longer into the night. Not hearing anything from his friend that was following her didn't help either and he didn't have the heart to call and ask if he had any news.

In his head he felt that no news might just be good news. In his heart he knew this wouldn't be the case. He braced for the worst and hoped for the best, it was all he could do at this point. Although he had to admit that the waiting and not knowing was killing him inside.

A week later his friend called and said they had to meet. Ted was beside himself with fear the worst was about to happen. When he met his friend, he learned that his fears were warranted. There on the table in front of him were pictures proving Elaine's infidelity.

They showed the mystery man meeting her at his front door with a kiss. His friend had even managed to get close enough to the house to get some very incriminating photos of the two of them in bed together. Ted's world as he knew it just came crumbling down around him and all he could do was shake his head in disbelief.

He could do nothing but take the pictures and tell his friend thanks for finally getting to the bottom of this for him. He was numb and felt as though that beam had just dropped on him again. He was crushed and wasn't sure what his next move would be or should be.

If he followed his heart, he would go home and throw everything she owned onto the front lawn and change the locks on the doors. He knew this would accomplish nothing and decided not to be childish about this. He had to act like an adult and confront her once and for all with the proof he now had.

When she returned home from work, she found him sitting in the kitchen at the table. He had a rather large manilla envelope in front of him and had a look she had never seen on his face. "What's wrong,,, are the kids ok?" she asked with a definite concern in her voice.

He couldn't bring himself to say a word, he just pushed the envelope over to her and watched as she opened it. She became the palest white and just dropped the pictures back onto the table. "Where did you get these?" she asked.

He told her that he had hired a private detective to put his fears and suspicions to rest once and for all. Little did he know that instead of feeling like a fool, he found that his fears had been right all along.

She broke down and cried uncontrollably and could only say "I'm sorry" over and over. "Where did we go wrong Elaine?" he asked. They talked into the night and she filled in all the blanks he still had left. She had met this man, Lou, at work and at first it was nothing more than a friend lending an ear and a shoulder to cry on.

He told her he knew that most of this was his fault for pushing her away after his accident. They actually sat there and discussed this like grown ups. He expected a lot of yelling and accusing and passing blame back and forth. Instead he got some honest answers to questions he was afraid to ask in the first place.

Soon the only question left unanswered was where they went from this point. Should they try to work things out and put this all behind them? Should they just chalk it up as a very bad decision on her part and forgive and forget? Ted was willing to work through this and save their marriage.

He still loved her with all his heart and did not want to throw that away. He had seen the changes come over her lately and knew that she wasn't the same person he married all those years ago. He had only hoped it was her way of growing up and facing their problem's head on. It wasn't.

They sat up and talked most of the evening and Ted got some answers he wasn't fully prepared for. He quickly learned that her friendship with this man became physical just a few months ago and she had fallen madly and hopelessly in love with this man.

She couldn't explain it nor did she really want to. She knew this was killing Ted inside but right now, she could only think of her own feelings. That seemed to bother him more than anything, she was only worried about her feelings and this Lou guy.

She told Ted that she had no intentions of giving this man up and working things out between them. She had in fact been looking for a much gentler, kinder way to tell him. She didn't want him finding out like this. That was never her intent.

She still loved Ted and probably always would, but she had changed. They both had since his accident. She took him by surprise when she offered to pack her things and leave him with the house. He fully expected her to ask him to leave and he was prepared to do just that. He hadn't expected her to offer to move out and give him the house instead.

She even called in sick the next day so they could work this out like adults and come to some sort of common ground between them. Of course, her "friend" Lou called her cell phone to see what was wrong with her. Her new love got a shock when Ted answered the call instead.

The man was brazen enough to ask who he was and ask where Elaine was though. "He couldn't be that stupid" Ted thought as he told the man he was her husband. "Oh, it's you" was the only response he got.

Ted wasn't about to pass up an opportunity like this and let the man have it with both barrels. Elaine was in the shower so he didn't have to pull any punches with this idiot when it came to telling him exactly how he felt and what he thought of this guy.

It felt rather good to let this man know that he had intruded on a love and marriage that had lasted more than twenty-five years. Ted made sure he knew that he was the reason they were going to split up and wind up in a divorce court instead of a marriage counselors office.

Nothing Ted said to this mindless little moron seemed to get through. He only said "uh huh" once in a while and seemed to ignore anything else Ted said. When Ted was done the only thing the man said was "just tell her I called."

Ted was beside himself at this point. He wanted nothing more than to drive over to her job, drag this sixty's reject out of that warehouse and stomp him into a little puddle right in front of everyone there. He also knew that although he would feel great, it would only push Elaine closer to this guy.

That was the last thing in the world he wanted to do right now, push her any further away than she already was. He told the man that he would give her the message and hung up. Elaine heard him talking to someone and asked who had called.

His first thought was to tell her one of the guys called that he used to work with to see how he was doing. But lying to her would only put him down to her level and right now he would be damned if he would give her that satisfaction. He told her the truth that her new boyfriend had called and was worried because she had missed work.

She broke down and cried and told him how very sorry she was that he had called. She told him that she knew this was tearing him up inside and that she knew he would like nothing more than to go over there and beat the guy to a bloody pulp. She also asked him, she didn't tell him, she asked him, not to. He told her that he wasn't about to waste his time on someone as insignificant as that guy.

In his heart he wanted nothing more than to break that promise to her. **In his head he knew that twisting this guy into knots would** accomplish nothing more than to make her want to be with him more. He just wanted to choke the life out of this guy right now for ruining what they had worked so hard for so long to accomplish. He also knew that he had to be the bigger person right now and respect her wishes to let go and leave it alone. They spent most of that day working all the details on the split.

Chapter 11

Ted spent the next couple of weeks avoiding her like the plague and looking at apartments. He thought he found one that would fulfill his needs nicely when he got a call from his old boss. He told Ted that he had just bought this little house and it needed some minor repairs if Ted might be interested in making some extra money.

Of course he jumped at the chance and took down the address. He told his friend that he would go right over and take a look at it and let him know what he thought. His friend told Ted that if the house looked like it needed more than it would be worth, he didn't need to sugarcoat it for him. Ted said he wouldn't and his friend knew that he could trust Ted to be both fair and honest.

As he pulled up in front of the little house he immediately noticed how lonely and out of place it looked. It was surrounded by newer, sprawling, massive homes and it looked almost helpless and lonely sitting there all by itself. He quickly wondered how it had escaped being torn down to make room for the massive homes surrounding it.

Ted had been told where to find a key to gain access and once inside, he fell in love with the old home. It was a two bedroom, one bath, white frame house. It had a detached two car garage joined to the house by a breeze way. He quickly found his way to the basement and inspected the foundation. It was as solid as the day it had been built. He could only think how they don't build houses today like they did when this house was built.

He took a notepad and pencil in and quickly started jotting down notes. Quickly finding things he thought needed attention and what he thought it might cost. When he had all his measurements and figures in order, he called his friend back with his findings.

His old boss asked Ted for his honest opinion, and asked it he thought the home worth fixing up or should it just be torn down and sold for the land. Ted asked what he intended to do with the house and his friend said he wasn't really sure at this point.

It appears that he bought the house for nearly nothing and wasn't sure whether to repair it and rent the house out or tear it down and sell the land. Either way he would recoup his money and come out of the deal in good shape.

It was then that Ted asked if they could meet face to face. He told his friend that he had a proposition for him. He told his friend that he might have a way to do both, fix it up and rent it at the same time. They agreed to meet for lunch and Ted quickly jumped in his truck and drove off.

They met at a local restaurant they often went to, to discuss work plans and things. The regulars where glad to see Ted as he hadn't been there since his accident. He and his friend quickly found a table where they could talk with some degree of privacy.

Ted filled him in on what was going on between him and Elaine and swore him to secrecy as no one knew about it yet. His friend told him he would never repeat a word of their conversation but told him how surprised he was as well.

Ted quickly laid out his plan to his friend for him to rent the house, as he needed to find a place of his own soon anyway. He told him that he just fell in love with the little place the minute he pulled up in front of it. He even offered to sweeten the pot, so to speak, and offered to do all the needed repairs out of his own money.

He told his friend that the labor could be exchanged for some free rent instead. He went on to say that if he could afford it, he would just buy the little house from him. But, told his friend that saving the money would take a little time.

His friend quickly agreed to his proposal but this time his friend sweetened the pot. He informed Ted that he had been meaning to call him anyway as they really needed to sit down and talk. It appears that after Ted left the company and settled with the insurance company, they all overlooked a rather large detail.

Ted had been enrolled in and participating in the companies 401K program as well as their stock purchase program since they started them. A fact they had all overlooked. He told Ted that after looking over some papers he found recently, he discovered that Ted had a rather considerable sum of money in the companies 401K and owned a large share of the company's stock.

As they sat and ate lunch Ted soon discovered that he had a small financial windfall that had been totally forgotten about and overlooked, until now. His friend told him that he would buy the materials needed to fix the little house up. He didn't want Ted to pay for materials out of his own pocket. He really didn't think that sounded fair to Ted.

He would rent the house to Ted and would exchange Ted's labor for the monthly rent for the time being. He knew that if Ted and Elaine went through a divorce it could get messy and a bit sticky if her attorney found out about the money he had forgotten about in his 401K. So for time being, they would just forget that existed.

It was quickly agreed that Ted would take immediate possession of the tiny house and move in as soon as he wanted. They would trade rent for labor in fixing the old place up. After the divorce was final and all the smoke cleared, they would meet again and discuss the situation again in more detail.

They would sit down and go into more detail how much money Ted actually had coming to him afterwards. "It might just be enough to buy that little place from me with a good chunk left over" his friend told him. He liked the sound of that, having his own place and it being fully paid for.

They shook hands and agreed upon a verbal agreement for time being. If nothing was put on paper, nothing could be used against Ted in court. He felt a bit guilty about concealing this from Elaine, but then again, she had concealed quite a lot from him lately hadn't she?

He quickly thanked his friend and told him that he would start moving things in right away. They agreed that a change of locks would be in order and his friend said he would have that taken care of before the end of the day. He told Ted the new keys would be in the same spot he found the old ones and to come and go as he pleased.

It was friends like this that Ted was happy to have. He was glad they decided to stand beside him and not question or judge, just help.

He quickly went home and started loading all of his tools into his truck. The place did need some repairs and in order to do them he would need his tools.

His timing was impeccable. Just as he was returning to the house with his tools the locksmith was finishing up with his task of installing the new locks. He gave Ted the new keys and Ted went about placing his tools in the garage.

It was the first step in moving out and letting Elaine have what she said she wanted, her new life with her new love. It was painful, but a first step he knew he had to take. He knew their marriage was over and she had been very clear about what she wanted. He was going to respect her wishes and give it to her without hesitation or reservation.

He loved her enough to let her go. And let her go he would do. He would start by moving his things into the new house little by little. He saw no reason to make a large production of him moving out. He decided to keep it rather low key and would tell only Elaine for now.

It wouldn't do anyone any good to make a big deal over this and start drawing those lines in the sand that he didn't want drawn in the first place. He would tell her as soon as she came home from work today and let her know that his things would slowly but steadily disappear from the house. He made a quick stop by one of the local supermarkets and picked up some boxes so he could start packing.

As soon as Elaine was in the house and settled for the moment, he told her of finding his own place and about his plans on moving things out gradually. She was grateful that he wasn't going to make a huge deal about this. She, like him, didn't want to air their laundry in public and thought it best that the fewer that knew, the better.

She helped him pack with tears steadily streaming down her cheeks. She knew that it was killing him inside as well, but she also knew this was something she had said she wanted. She only hoped that she was making the right choice and right now, it didn't seem like it at all. Right now it seemed like the dumbest idea she had ever had.

She had been through so much with this man. They had been through so much together. How could she just turn her back on him now and watch as he packed? Ready to move out of her house and out of her life forever. She was suddenly second guessing herself. She was suddenly thinking that she should call Lou and tell him to leave her alone and beg Ted to stay.

What if this new man in her life got tired of her and bored with her? Would he stand beside her like she knew Ted would? Or would he simply toss her by the wayside and move onto his next conquest? With each item of Ted's she packed she could think of a hundred reasons to beg him to forgive her.

She knew though that Ted was a proud man and wouldn't come back and go away every time she snapped her fingers. She knew that once his mind was made up, no one could change it but him. It appeared to her now, that his mind was clearly made up and he wasn't about to change it. Not now or anytime soon.

He was packing to move to a new place of his own. One without her. He would start a new life by himself as she selfishly started her new one with a man she chose over him. He was handling this exactly as she expected him to do, with grace and composure. He was letting her go because she wanted him to.

Packing wasn't as big a task as one would expect. Although they had accumulated much together, he decided to take little with him. He was going to let her have nearly everything and wanted it that way. He would take some of the spare furniture and one of the bedroom sets from the kids' old rooms.

They had extra televisions and stereos and had even acquired an extra set of dishes and pot and pans along the way. She made sure he would have everything he needed to set up his new place. She wasn't about to keep anything from him that he might need or want to take.

As soon as the packing was done and everything securely in boxes, he went in and started dinner. He decided it best to wait till dark to move any of his things as he didn't want the neighbors in the middle of all this. She agreed and even offered to go with him and help him unload the truck.

"No matter what happens between us Ted, I will always love you and want you in my life in some way" she told him as they sat down to eat. He assured her that he understood this and would not shut her out either. For the most part, they ate in silence.

After dinner was done, dishes cleared off and everything put away, it was dark enough to load the truck. Elaine did as she said she would do and rode along to help him take things into his new place. She just loved the house and was glad that he wasn't going to be living in some dump somewhere.

She had been afraid that he just wouldn't care and would take anything he could find no matter how bad it was. She was glad he chose such a nice little place. It even had a garage for him to store his tools in and do little projects.

After the boxes where in he gave her a tour of the house. She said she would put some more things together for him like family pictures and other items she knew he would need. He thanked her and they drove back home in silence.

As they each got ready for bed she asked if he would be completely moved by tomorrow or would he take his time? She told him there was no need to hurry but she knew he would want to be out as soon as possible.

He told her he would get things moved as quickly as he could but might wait till he got some of the repairs done the house needed to move any big items in. She told him to take his time and told him goodnight as she went to her room.

He had been sleeping in one of the kids' old rooms the last few weeks anyway so it wasn't like he thought that tonight would be the last time he would feel her next to him. He decided to sleep in one of the spare rooms right after she told him she wasn't going to leave her new love and stay with him.

He knew that sleeping alone was something he would have to get used to anyway, so he started it right away. Besides, how could he sleep in the same bed with her knowing what he now knew? He just couldn't bring himself to do that.

He couldn't bear the thought of her next to him knowing she was sleeping with another man. He didn't think she expected him to and thought that might be the reason she didn't fight him in his decision to use separate beds. He told her goodnight as he closed the door and prepared for bed himself.

He knew the next week or so would be busy and full for him. The little house he was moving into needed to have some minor repairs done before he would move furniture and big items into it. This would take the biggest part of his days and since working a full day wasn't something he was accustomed to, he was sure he would sleep well at night.

He hadn't been sleeping very well since moving into a room by himself. He could hear Elaine in her room and hear every move she made and every sound. It was all he could do not to open her door and join her. Hoping this all would be a very bad dream and they would awake and be like old times again. He knew that was not going to happen but in the back of his mind, he wanted it to.

As he lay in bed staring at the ceiling, he could hear Elaine in her room and hear that she was crying. He wanted so badly to go in and just take her in his arms and hold her. He also knew that he couldn't allow himself to do that. If he did, he would never find the courage to walk away and start his own life.

She had made her choice, even if he thought it was the wrong one. It was one he was going to respect and live with. She would get used to him not being there any longer. He was sure her new man would fill her evenings soon enough.

Before she realizes it, he will be a distant memory and she will have a new life with a new man. He just hoped that this guy would not use her and toss her away. He wasn't sure he would be able to allow her back into his life to help her pick up the pieces if that happened.

He wasn't sure if he would really ever be able to fully trust her again after all this. He also knew that if she did get hurt, he would at least be there as a friend. He would never turn his back on her completely. That just wasn't in him.

Soon he was fast asleep and morning came much quicker than he wanted it to. He quickly got up, showered and gathered his things to leave. He looked at the clock and noticed it was already seven o'clock. He had slept in this morning as he was usually up before Elaine left for work and she leaves around six every morning.

Just then he heard a sound come from the direction of her room. He slowly opened the door and saw her sitting on the bed. It seemed that she was looking for a reason not to go to work this morning or wanting him to rush in and beg her to change her mind. He wasn't about to do that and simply asked if she were ok.

She said she just forgot to set her alarm and would be on her way soon. He told her to have a good day and said he would probably not be there tonight for dinner. He told her he wanted to get as much done at the house today as possible and would probably just pick up something and eat there. She told him to be careful and to have a good day himself before he closed the door and left. She then broke down and cried uncontrollably as she tried to get herself for work.

For Better, For Worse?

Chapter 12

Over the next couple of weeks the days seemed to pass quickly. Ted was busy getting the house ready to move in to and time seemed to get away from him some days. He buried himself in that house and soon it was ready for furniture and the remaining items he was leaving at Elaine's.

He had even slept a couple of nights at the house so he could get an early start and finish as fast as possible. He was actually getting a bit anxious to move in completely and start his new life. He wasn't looking forward to starting it alone. He was just kind of excited about moving on and letting Elaine have her own space.

He knew that if she and this new guy were going to get off on the right foot, sneaking around was not the way to do it. With him finally gone, she would be able to come and go as she pleased without fear of running into him.

Now she could start spending time with her new man and he could start dropping by and spending time with her as well. He felt like a third wheel most of time anymore anyway even if it was just him and Elaine at the house.

She had never openly dishonored or disrespected him by bringing this guy around while he was there. He had to at least give her that much credit. She at least thought enough of him to go to his house and not flaunt him in Ted's face.

He picked up the rest of his things and furniture while she was at work. He thought it best to do it that way. He really wasn't looking forward to anymore encounters with her as he feared he would back out at the last minute and never leave.

And leaving was something he knew he had to do. She had made in abundantly clear that she was going to continue seeing this man and he couldn't live her while she did. Leaving was the only answer.

By now most of their friends and neighbors knew that something was wrong. They had seen him picking up things and leaving during the day and knew that wasn't like him. They just assumed that Ted

Page 73

had decided to move on his own and was leaving Elaine.

They felt so sorry for her and he let them believe this was all his fault. If asked he would just say that this was something he had to do and leave it at that. He wasn't even sure any more why he was still protecting her.

He could very easily have just told the truth and let all her friends know what kind of woman she really was. Instead he chose to let her save face and take the blame himself.

He had finally sat down with Mandy and Kyle and told them what was going on. They both noticed something was wrong but didn't realize the level of seriousness it had reached until their dad explained it. Ted even had a nice long phone conversation with Tommy so he didn't hear it from someone else. He wanted it to come from him.

With all his things finally moved into the new house he contacted his attorney to finalize everything. He filed for divorce shortly after moving and everyone thought he was a cruel and heartless bastard for doing this to her. He and the kids knew the truth and as far as he was concerned, that was good enough.

Ted let them think what they wanted and knew in his heart this was the final step in a process she started by cheating. He had to put a period to all this if he wanted any kind of life of his own. He and his attorney thought this would be a very simple and amicable procedure, only to find a fight they weren't expecting.

Out of the blue, Elaine became very bitter, cold, and almost greedy. Wanting to get anything she could from Ted. She wanted to leave him with nothing. He could only guess it was from prodding of her new love Lou.

He knew that she would never have thought about being this combative and vindictive on her own. He was sure her new boyfriend was behind this and that made the urge for him to pay the little moron a visit even greater. Once again though he showed composure and restraint and left well enough alone.

After dragging out for nearly a year, the divorce was final and he could move on. Ted was beginning to think it would never be over.

Every time he and his attorney worked out a compromise, her attorney would come back with a new demand from her. It was enough to make Ted want to scream.

He was just thankful that it was negotiated between attorneys and wasn't being drug out in court. That really would have aired the dirty laundry and it would be hers for the whole town to see. After the fight she drug him through he was to the point where he didn't care any longer if the whole world knew what she had done to him.

In the end an agreement was reached and Ted had even gotten word that her boyfriend had backed off and was remaining silent through the remainder of the proceedings. Ted had suspicions that someone had gotten to him and told him to keep his big mouth shut but could never prove it. He only wished if that were the case that he knew so he could thank them properly.

Just a feeling that he felt in his gut and it would make perfect sense. After he backed off and shut up, the rest of the procedure went as smooth as silk. The one and only time they did appear in court was the day the decree was declared final. Ted could not believe his eyes. She had enough nerve to bring her new boyfriend Lou to court with her. That day, of all days.

As they exited the courtroom, now officially divorced, Ted couldn't resist. He walked over to Elaine, took her in his arms and kissed her deeply and passionately. He kissed her with such passion her knees buckled. He held her tight so she wouldn't fall to the floor.

He then told her he only wished the best for her and told her goodbye. As he turned to leave her new man Lou jumped in front of him and stuck his finger in Ted's face. "Don't ever lay your hands on my woman again" the little punk told him. Ted couldn't hold back any longer.

He grabbed him by the throat, slammed him against the wall and simply smiled at him. "First of all, don't ever get in my face again." "If you ever do, remember this, I still know lots of people in construction." "They are digging foundations and pouring concrete every day, you can and will simply disappear, got it dumb-ass?"

With that Ted put the little dork down, brushed him off and continued. "If you hurt her, I will find you and no one will ever see or hear from you again, understand me punk?" He went on to say, "that is not an idle threat, it's a bonafide promise" and walked away.

Kyle was there and saw his dad straighten the dork out and patted him on the back and said "lets go have a beer dad." Of course Kyle was also behind his dad as he held the creep by the throat saying "let me dad, let me do it." He would have been happy to do that for his dad. He turned his back on his mom and simply left.

That wasn't something that Ted wasn't going to allow to happen. He would not see her children turn their backs on her. She had made a mistake and made some wrong choices, but, she still didn't deserve that. He and Kyle walked down the hall and disappeared through the door. That would be the last time Elaine would see Ted or her son for some time.

As they sipped their beer, Ted's attorney joined them. He told them that her attorney had asked the guy if he wanted to press charges and he refused. Ted was sorry for what he had done but couldn't resist the urge to get in one shot at the man that ruined his family and changed his life forever.

For that, it would have been worth any fine or time in jail he would have to spend. His attorney asked what he was going to do now and Ted could only say, "start over." As they gathered their things to leave his attorney wished him all the luck and Kyle asked "where to now dad?"

Ted asked his son if he would like to stop over and see his new place. He hadn't had anyone over since he had moved in and knew it was time his son got a look at the place. Kyle agreed and said he would love to see what his dad had done to the place. They all knew that he had been working on the house.

They went to their trucks and Kyle followed his dad to his new home. He was amazed at what his dad had done with the place already. It wasn't finished but was in much better shape than the first day Ted had seen it.

Kyle immediately offered to stop by one or two evenings and give his dad a hand with the finishing touches. "I would like that son" he told Kyle. Kyle got a complete tour of the little house and just loved it. He was glad his dad had found what he could call a new home. Even more glad that it gave him a project to take his mind off all the things going on with his mom.

He just couldn't believe that she would do something like this to his dad. He lost a lot of respect for her when he found out what was really going on. As Kyle got ready to leave, he asked his dad if there was anything he needed before he left.

Ted assured his son that he was fine and didn't need anything. "I love you dad" he said as he hugged his dad and opened the door. "I love you too son" Ted said as his son walked to his truck.

He actually was looking forward to Kyle giving him a hand finishing the house. He was glad his son wanted to be involved in his project. The work he had done so far was nothing major or too involved. Mostly just replacing wore out things and paint and patching a few blemishes here and there.

The outside of the home only needed a fresh coat of paint and some attention to the yard. Before long Ted had the showcase of the neighborhood and all his neighbors just adored the work he had done so far. They were all so happy that he was taking such pride in the old house. Most of them wondered what would ever become of it.

He had made it a point to meet his neighbors and get to know each one. They were happy to have him in the neighborhood and everyone enjoyed his company immensely. The new friends he had made while performing the work to the house had invited him to backyard cookouts and even asked his opinion on some minor repairs they needed in their own homes.

He was soon one of the most well liked and popular guys on the block. During the months the fight over the divorce drug out he even picked up some odd jobs from the neighbors and was able to put a little money away for a rainy day. He was settling in and before long he was a familiar part of their little community.

Time had passed quickly and gotten away from him from time to time. Mandy and her husband Dan already had one child with another on the way and due anytime. Kyle and his wife Erica had one and another due in the fall. The woman Tommy married Debbie, already had two little girls and they loved him as if he was their own dad.

He was a grandpa and single again and more dazed and confused most of the time than anything. It was his kids and grandchildren that kept him from going totally crazy during all the turmoil. He was truly blessed to have them in his life.

Now that Kyle had seen the place, he decided it was time to do some entertaining of his own. He called and invited Mandy, Kyle and their families over to see his house this weekend and they would grill out and make a day of it. They said they could hardly wait and Kyle stopped a couple of days that week to lend a helping hand in a couple of projects his dad had going at the house.

Life was marching on. He was doing it on his own without Elaine and the world hadn't stopped turning. And, the end of the world as we know it was not nearing. Maybe he would get through this in better shape than he had ever imagined he thought to himself.

After Kyle left, he picked up a few lose branches from the yard, locked the garage and decided to call it an early night. He entered the house, grabbed a soda from the refrigerator and turned on the TV.

One of his favorite shows were just coming on, so, he decided some rest and relaxation were the order of the evening. Just then the phone rang, fully expecting it to be Kyle or Mandy he picked up and said hello. To his surprise it was his friend, his old boss, on the other end.

"Ted you old son of a gun" he said, "how are things with you?" Ted told him that everything was good, though he did tell his friend about court today and the run in he had with her little playmate. His friend said he wished he had been there to see that.

They talked about the house and he asked if Ted needed anything in the way of materials or anything. His friend knew that Ted was getting very close to being done with the little house and also knew that he had done a far better job than he could have ever imagined. "Stop by my office tomorrow Ted, we have some things to talk about" he said.

Ted quickly asked if there was a problem or something with the house. His friend quickly put his mind at ease by reminding him of the talk they had over a year ago during lunch. Ted told him that he had actually forgotten about that talk and would stop by in the morning.

As he settled back in his chair to watch his show, the conversation they had came back to him. "My old 401K and those stocks" Ted said to himself. "I completely forgot about that." He wondered just how much he even had coming.

He honestly hoped it might be enough to make his friend an offer on his little house. He would love nothing more than to pay buy it outright and not owe a dime on it. He had come to love that house in the year he had already been here. And the neighborhood was an absolute dream come true.

It was quiet yet everyone looked out for everyone else and it couldn't be a better place for him. He would just have to go talk to his friend tomorrow and see how much of a windfall he had coming. He was finding it hard to stay awake and knew that tomorrow would be a full day, so he turned everything off and headed for bed.

Morning seemed to come quickly, he headed straight for the shower. Of course that was after he put a pot of coffee on and took a pain pill. All the walking and steps at the courthouse yesterday had taken a toll on his poor knees. After a couple of cups of "wake me up" he called to make sure his friend would be in his office and headed out the door.

He was greeted with hugs and "how have you been" as soon as he entered the door. It was times like this that he fully realized just how much he missed this place, and the people. He knocked on his bosses door and was quickly told to come in. "Would you like a cup of coffee Ted?" his friend asked.

After coffee was delivered to them, he sat Ted down at the conference table and started laying out papers. "What is all this?" Ted asked. His friend went over all the paperwork with him and he soon discovered that he had much more money coming to him than he had ever dreamed possible.

After all, he had been with the company for over twenty years and had been putting money in the fund for most of that time. Not to mention the portion the company matched and added as well. The bottom line was Ted had a lot of money due him.

Then his friend made him an offer he couldn't refuse. He offered to buy the stock Ted owned in the company back from him and sell him the house for exact same amount. He told Ted this way we both get something out of the deal. You get the house and I get a large share of my company back.

It couldn't be called a trade but no actual money would exchange hands in the deal. His boss would just buy his stock back and draft papers to sell him the house for the exact same amount. In all actuality it was an even trade, it just couldn't be shown that way on paper.

They worked through all the details and soon everything was worked out. Ted would get a clear title to the house and a rather large check mailed to him from the balance due him from his 401K. It was a good day indeed he thought as he said his goodbyes and headed home.

Chapter 13

___During the course of the next couple of months a lot of things happened and happened fast. Ted received the title to the house and all the paperwork was finalized giving him total ownership. A check arrived in the mail from his 401K and he had elected to have taxes deducted so the money was his, free and clear.

Tommy and his family came home on leave and Kyle and Mandy were over almost daily. It was a busy time yet good time. He and Kyle had put all the finishing touches on the house and it was not only paid for and his, but completely finished as well.

Ted had invited Elaine over for dinner while Tommy and everyone were there. Of course he met a little more than subtle objections from his children but after a heart to heart talk with everyone they agreed to include their mom in their dinner plans.

Ted merely explained to his children that like it or not she was still their mother and always would be. It was no different than the both of them standing behind them and their decisions even if they didn't like them or agree with them.

She had made mistakes but all of us make mistakes. And although they all might disagree with the choices she made, they all still had to love her and support her. She would always be there to love and support each and every one of them and they owed her the same in return. She was still their mother.

After his sermon, they all agreed that their dad was right. She was still their mom and she still loved them and always would. No matter what they did or how wrong they might be, she would always be there for them and they knew it.

They agreed with their dad to forgive and forget and accept her and her choices without judgement. He was glad that he could reason with his children about Elaine being included in their plans. He knew they were hurt over all of this too. He also knew deep down they loved their mom. They were just still mad at her for what had happened.

That first dinner in his new house marked the beginning of him including Elaine in all the gatherings they had. It was then that he decided to hide his feelings and make sure she remained a very big part of all of their lives. She was after all their mother and deserved that much.

She didn't do anything to them personally. What had happened between him and Elaine was exactly that, between them. He loved his children with his very being but also knew there were times and things that would not directly involve them and this was one of them.

He and their mom tried and failed to save their marriage, it really was that simple. It wasn't all her and it wasn't all him. It was both of them and there was no point in her being the escape goat catching the brunt of their anger for what had happened.

After hearing their dad explain things like this they all agreed it was time to be a family again and family included mom. Elaine later found out that his sermon was the pivotal point of the children accepting her back into their lives. She didn't know that at first but all three of her children pulled her aside and made sure she knew it was Ted that made them see the light.

She was always grateful to him for doing this for her. Although she really wasn't sure why he would want to after all she had put him through. She just accepted it and decided from the start never to do anything that would reverse his decision to include her in family gatherings. She was also smart enough to know that these gatherings would never include her new boyfriend Lou.

Elaine had done some terrible things lately and pushing Ted and the kids away for another man was one of the dumbest. She wasn't about to jeopardize their letting her back in now for anything. If that meant she had to attend these occasions without her new boyfriend, then she was willing to do it. She knew that bringing him would only cause trouble and that was the last thing she wanted now.

She also knew that if she started bringing him around it would not only drive the children away again, but, would keep her isolated from her grandchildren as well. She wasn't about to do anything that would cause that, now or ever. She loved her children and grandchildren and a huge hole formed in her heart the day they turned their backs on her after the divorce.

If Ted could reason with them and get them to allow her back in their lives, she would respect their feelings and be on her best behavior. Besides, her boyfriend knew that he was neither welcome nor wanted around the family and knew that there would be times that gatherings would not include him.

He might be a moron but he wasn't a complete idiot either and knew if he pushed the issue, he wouldn't like the outcome. Some said Elaine let him control her like a puppet on a string, and they might be right to an extent. However, this guy had also seen her fury and temper first hand and knew that if push came to shove, he would back off and fast.

The next few months found Elaine being included in everything. Birthdays, family cookouts, Holidays and special occasions that they had always shared together. It was like old times, at times. Ted was the one that died inside each time an evening like these came to an end. He would watch her leave knowing she wasn't coming back until the next gathering and it just killed him.

Before everyone knew it Mandy and Kyle both had their new arrivals and Ted and Elaine couldn't be prouder or happier grandparents. Good times had returned, as much as they could under the circumstances, to the family. Tommy and his wife made a huge announcement as well.

Tommy and his wife were going to have a little boy. They waited until they were sure of her pregnancy and the sex of the child before they told everyone. "Looks like you're going to get your boy after all" Ted told his son upon receiving the news. They couldn't be happier for them or for each other as this would bring the grandchild count to nine.

The rest of that year past without much commotion or anything out of the ordinary happening. Tommy and his wife had a beautiful little baby boy and all was well with the world for the time being. Ted and Elaine shared many a moment together fussing over the new arrival and to those that didn't know any better, it would appear they were still together.

The following year would bring some rather large and unwelcome changes as Elaine finally announced that she was going to marry this Lou guy. Even some of her closest friends warned her that they thought this to be a disaster waiting to happen but she ignored everyone. Ted finally saw that any shred of hope he ever had for the two of them getting back together was now gone.

Of course Elaine wanted her children and grandchildren to be happy for her and come to the wedding. She even asked if the kids would be in the wedding party. Of course they all turned to their dad and asked what they should do. He could only tell them to follow their hearts on this one. "Just don't do anything that you'll regret later" he told them.

Elaine was heartbroken when they unanimously decided they would not be in her wedding or at it. She of course could understand how they felt and didn't want to ruin the bond she had built with them over the last year or so. She also knew that Ted would not intervene this time and give another sermon. She was pretty sure he would agree with them wholeheartedly this time.

She knew deep in her heart that this would be seen as the final betrayal by her toward him. She wasn't about to cause a scene and look even worse in the eyes of her friends, family or children. She decided it best to accept the way they felt and go on with her plans without them. She was still their mother and would continue to be a big part of their lives, she would do nothing to put that in peril.

Elaine was married in a small and very private ceremony and soon her new husband moved in officially to her house. Everyone just guessed that he decided to move in with her as her home was nearly paid for. Even some of those that stood beside her and sided against Ted were seeing her in a new light.

Because of her new husband her old friends were soon pushed out as they really didn't accept him or like him and he knew it. He decided for her that his friends were better for them and hers could go back to being friends with her ex. She became more than a little distant once more, even to Ted and the kids after her marriage.

Ted always told the kids to give her some space, "it takes time to work out the bugs in a new relationship, you all know that" he told them. They all knew he was right, they had experienced it themselves right after marriage and it took a little time to work out the kinks. They just shrugged it off as a phase and knew she would start including herself again when she felt comfortable.

They all seemed to be right, soon Elaine was including herself once again in gatherings and family happenings. It seemed that her "adjustment period" was finally over and she once again seemed like her old self.

For the most part, things were as back to normal as they get in situations like this. Elaine was part of the family again, if only for gatherings, and they were all together and happy again. As happy as they could be anyway.

The months passed and Ted soon knew that any hope he had been hanging on to in regards to him and Elaine ever getting back together were long gone. He knew in his heart it was time to finally move on with his own life and stop hoping she would come back. It was a sad and heartbreaking time for him, but an adjustment he knew he had to make.

It was time to put Elaine where she belonged, in his past. They were not going to get back together and she had moved on. He had to start a new chapter in his life and decided there was no time like the present. Besides, his kids and friends were still subtly trying to play matchmaker from time to time. Maybe it was time for him to stop saying no and just meet some new people.

He thought at the very least he might meet some interesting new friends and one can never really have too many of those. He was going to do it. He was going to start dating again. It scared him to death to even think of the concept but he knew it was time. The next time someone tried to "fix him up" he would just say sure. At the worst, he would end up alone for the rest of his life and alone was something he was becoming accustomed to anyway.

After the divorce he really never gave any serious thought to starting a new life with a new person like Elaine had done. That really didn't appeal to him and wasn't something that he was looking forward to. After all, Elaine had done it and she didn't seem to have any trouble adjusting to new people and new things. If she could do it, so could he.

It wasn't long and he was being approached by friends and the kids about getting out of that house and doing something. Unlike the past, he accepted their offers to find him dates. Everyone was elated as they only had his best interests at heart.

They just didn't want to see him lonely and alone any longer. They loved him and he knew it. He knew they were only looking out for him and only wanted what was best for him in the long run.

It seemed like only a day or two but in all actuality it was several weeks later and he was preparing to go on his first date. It was a friend of one of his friends that was a widow. He had already met her at his friend's house, so, this was no blind date. He was nervous and couldn't figure out why.

After all, they were only going to dinner and maybe a movie if the dinner went well. He wasn't prepared to make any plans past dinner as he wasn't really sure just how comfortable he would be. Or her for that matter.

They might find out that they have absolutely nothing in common and are totally incompatible and want to call it an early evening. He left himself an out by suggesting dinner and then they would see where things went from there.

The lady he was meeting was more agreeable to it than he thought she might be as she too was a bit nervous herself. It seems that he would be her first date since her late husband had passed and she too was more than a little apprehensive.

They seemed like two junior high school kids on their first date with their parents sitting at the table next to them. Neither of them wanting to break the ice nor start a conversation they might regret starting later. It was almost comical. They miraculously made it through dinner and decided that movie wasn't out of the question after all. All in all it was an enjoyable evening.

The two went out several more times but in the end decided that remaining good friends appealed to them much more than anything else. Ted was glad he had found a new friend and she would be one he would keep the rest of his life.

She was the nicest lady he could ever hope to meet. They just weren't destined to be romantically involved and both knew it, and gladly accepted it. They both knew though that they were destined to be friends for a very long time and called each other all the time.

He did date several more times and met an array of very interesting and attractive ladies. He was having fun and glad he was getting out of the house. Just nothing he would consider life changing was becoming of it.

He actually caught himself more than once comparing the ladies he met to Elaine and he knew that was a horrible mistake. Maybe he would continue to do that for the rest of his life he thought to himself. And that scared him immensely. That wasn't fair to himself or the women he went out with.

Let's face it, if Elaine had been the perfect woman to compare them all to, he would still be with her now, wouldn't he? He knew that it wasn't fair to himself or his dates to compare them to her or anyone else for that matter. They were all individuals and their own person. They didn't compare and never would just like Elaine could never compare to any of the women he did date.

For the most part, Ted just resigned himself to the fact that he might just live the rest of his life alone. He wasn't really sure that it was what he wanted. But, he was quite sure that it would be ok and he would be fine if he did end up alone after all.

He was doing fine on his own now. He did have to learn to live on his own again that was tricky at times. Learning how to do laundry, cooking, cleaning, shopping for himself. It had all been a learning experience and he had weathered the storm just fine. He could do this he thought to himself. He could do this.

He had been doing it now for over a year and was doing just fine really. He had "offed" anyone with his cooking and his clothes were clean. The house was in order and he had even learned to shop for bargains and to use coupons. He was handling this single life just fine and could continue to do so.

Chapter 14

Time seemed to pass quickly and before he knew it three years had passed since he and Elaine's divorce. The kids and grandchildren were all doing well and in perfect health. He lost track of Elaine for a while. She seemed to distance herself once again from him and the rest of the family for some reason. He heard rumor that her and her new husband were having trouble but never gave it much merit. After all, rumors are just that, rumors.

He even found himself doing something he never thought he would do again, working, full time. It wasn't side jobs under the table for his old boss either. He had decided to take some of the money he received from his 401K and put it to use.

He formed his own construction business that specialized more in remodeling and things like that. He soon found work coming at him from everywhere and couldn't be happier. He was busy and life was moving forward.

His old boss did however hire him as a subcontractor on several projects. Before he knew it, he was hiring people and forming a crew of his own. Of course Kyle was the very first person he hired. He knew in his heart that in time he would leave his new business to Kyle and Tommy anyway.

What better way to teach Kyle the business than to let him help build it from the ground up he thought. It didn't take long for his reputation to spread like wildfire and before they knew it he and Kyle had more work than they knew what to do with.

They decided it was time to add more employees and equipment and become a full-fledged business in the Council Bluffs area. The community accepted them with open arms and soon they were not only well known but very successful as well.

Kyle couldn't be prouder of his dad for taking a giant leap like this and following a dream. It took a lot of guts and determination but Kyle knew his dad had plenty of both. He knew that leaving a job like he had and joining his dad was a leap as well, but one he was more than willing to take. He trusted his dad completely.

In just a short time they bought a parcel of land and built their own shop and office and were now a real business. Kyle's wife Erica went to work for them running the office and Mandy's husband Dan came aboard as well. Jobs were coming at them fast and before they knew it, they had enough work to keep them busy for a very long time.

It was fast becoming a true family owned and operated business and they couldn't be happier. Mandy of course stayed on at the school, they knew she would never leave her teaching behind. And Ted didn't expect her to either. To be honest he would have been more than a little disappointed if she had.

As the business grew and prospered something else unexpectedly happened to Ted. Elaine started coming around more and more. She was always stopping by jobs or dropping by his house for no apparent reason. She was staying later and later and seemed to be looking for a reason not to leave at all. It was if she were trying to involve herself in his life again. And in a very big way.

It didn't take him long to find out that her marriage was indeed in trouble and she was thinking of divorcing the man she had left him for. He could only smirk and think that justice might get served in this situation after all. He knew that it was a terrible thing to think but he just couldn't help himself.

She would now know what he went through and learn it firsthand and quickly. She would know how it felt to be tossed aside and wonder how someone you love can do something like that to you. Fate can be a real pain in the butt when she wants to be he thought to himself.

Of course he couldn't turn his back on her but at the same time, he wasn't about to welcome her with open arms back into his life either. The more she tried to include herself in his life the more he kept her at arms length away from it. He had made that mistake once and would not allow himself to let her back in now.

He was doing just fine on his own and liked it that way. He wasn't about to change things for her or anyone else for that matter, not at this point in his life. He had finally moved on and was building a life of his own. One that he was happy with, for now anyway. He still knew he didn't want to be alone the rest of his life. But, he knew that another chance with even her wasn't something he was willing to do right now either.

It had taken him a long time to be comfortable with things and how they happened. It took him countless hours of sleepless nights and rivers of tears to get her out of his system. He would be the best friend she ever hoped to have. But that was as much as he was willing to offer. He wasn't about to put himself or his children back through all that again, not for her or anyone else for that matter. He had his life now and was happy with it, just like it is.

It didn't take Elaine long to come out and ask him to take her back. She cried, she begged, she promised to never do anything as stupidly as she did before. She pleaded with him to let her come back to him. He had cried himself to sleep on many a night praying she would come to him and say those words.

Now here she was, saying the words he dreamed about so many times and all he could say was "no Elaine, I'm sorry." He couldn't believe the words had formed on his lips let alone actually escaped them. He couldn't believe that he was actually telling her he wasn't willing to take that chance again.

There he stood, holding her and remembering how right it felt and was telling her no. He just couldn't believe that he was really doing this. After some very long and lengthy talks she did finally say she understood and agreed that she would rather have him in her life as a friend than not at all.

He wasn't sure if she really meant it or it was just her way of hoping he would change his mind later. At this point he didn't honestly care. He would be her friend and help her in any way he could. He would just never allow himself to go back to her.

The rest of that year he poured himself into building the business. He and Elaine went out often to dinner, movies and even shopping. They were almost as close as they had been while they were married.

They just slept in separate beds in different locations. She soon filed for a divorce and had the fight of a lifetime on her hands.

He of course wanted to take everything she had and leave her both broke and alone. Ted was not going to stand by and watch that happen. Not because he was changing his mind about taking her back, but more because he hated the little moron she was getting rid of.

He was not about to stand idly by and watch this freeloading little twirp take her for everything he worked his butt off to give her. He secretly paid the guy a visit and shortly after, Lou decided it best if they made a clean break and go their separate ways.

Elaine always had a sneaky suspicion that Ted had talked to him but could never prove it. She was just glad to have it over and Ted stood beside her all the way through it. He turned out to be the best friend she had ever had and she was happy to still have that at least.

Ted did tell her that if she was going to make a clean break of it she would have to quit her job. She knew he was right, she didn't want to have to go to work every day and see the guy. After talking to Mandy, Kyle and Tommy he offered her a job with them until something else came along.

Of course his children made sure they quoted the same sermon to him that he used on them about her still being family to convince him to make that offer. He always knew those words would come back to bite him, and they did. He like them, knew they were right and saw the light after all.

They did have a valid point though, this was a family business and like it or not, she was still family. Ted just couldn't argue with reasoning like that. After all, it was him that instilled those values in his children in the first place.

Elaine took the offer and soon was working for him. They had her running parts to job sites and picking up parts and supplies from suppliers. She loved the job and was determined to show Ted he hadn't made a mistake by offering it to her.

Elaine loved her job and was so very proud of her ex-husband, and son. If anyone could make a success of this business, she just knew it would be Ted. He was a natural and Kyle was following in his dads footsteps splendidly. They saw each other all the time now and Elaine was at every gathering and holiday. She couldn't help but wonder in the back of her mind if Ted might change his mind and allow them another chance. She just knew it would work.

Ted stood fast on his decision not to attempt another go round with Elaine. He searched his heart and kept coming up with the same disturbing answer. He just couldn't trust her again. He still loved her like no tomorrow but not the kind of love that can make a marriage work.

She was the best friend he had ever had and he wanted to keep it that way. He was not going to get seriously involved with Elaine again. Even if it meant he would spend the rest of his life alone, he was prepared to do just that.

Several months passed and the business only seemed to thrive with each passing day. Ted and Kyle were always bidding new work and seemed to be constantly hiring new help. It was surpassing any of their wildest dreams and Ted could soon see that this business was one to take seriously. Even his old boss had commented that if things kept going, he might be working for Ted soon.

Ted passed it off as light hearted fun but knew in his heart that if they continued to grow at the pace they currently were, he might just be right. Elaine was working hard and things between them all seemed as normal as any family. Outsiders didn't know that Ted and Elaine were ex's.

They thought it was a husband and wife business and no one ever told them otherwise. It was a great year and the family seemed to thrive as much as the business. Good times had once again come into everyone's lives.

Mandy was being offered a promotion to Vice Principal and was seriously thinking of accepting the offer. Ted told her she could do so much more for those kids in a position like that and she knew he was right. He and Kyle were doing more wining and dining of major customers and the business was taking a turn toward the commercial

For Better, For Worse?

side of construction.

They would never stop doing what started them in the first place. But, the business seemed to be taking on a life all it's own and it was staggering to watch it. It was rapidly approaching the largest in town and Ted and Kyle couldn't be happier.

They were being awarded bigger and bigger jobs that paid more and more money. Tommy had even decided not to reenlist in the Navy so he could become more than a name on the business. He wanted to come home and have a hands on role in it.

Besides with his military experience and degrees it was making it easier and easier to land even government contracts. Elaine made an announcement that Ted never thought he would hear. Actually she approached him about buying their old house from her as she had decided to move.

He gladly accepted to buy the house and Tommy and his family was going to move into it as soon as they came home. Tommy said he couldn't think of a better place to raise his own kids than the house he was raised in. Everyone was glad that the house would be staying in the family.

Elaine announced that she was going to be moving out of state. She had family in southern Indiana and never did see enough of them. They only time they ever did see this part of the family was once a year for family reunions. And once a year for only a couple of days in never enough time to spend with family.

She thought that if moving on with her life wasn't going to include Ted, maybe she would have a better chance at starting over in a new area all together. Of course everyone including Ted was saddened to think that she wouldn't be there every day or just a phone call away.

He also knew that this might be the best move she ever made. Maybe she could build some kind of life for herself elsewhere. He wished her all the luck in the world and she promised to make as many gatherings and holidays as possible.

The kids were sad to think their mom was moving on and out of state but at the same time felt happy for her. They knew it would allow her a fresh start in a new place and that could only be a good thing for her. They knew she would keep her promise about being there as much as she possibly could and vowed to visit her as much as time allowed. It was a sad time but a happy time.

It was a time of closing doors permanently and opening new ones at the same time. It put an end to old lives and started new ones and everyone would be stronger and happier in the end. Ted and Kyle offered to load her things on one of the company's trucks and help her move down. She gladly accepted the offer as she wasn't looking forward to a moving company doing it for her. She was happy that they wanted to do this for her.

Ted and Kyle took a couple of days off and loaded her things on a truck and started off. She drove her car and they followed her all the way to Indiana. It gave Ted and Kyle time to see the family as well. And they liked that idea.

It was aunts, uncles and cousins that they saw only for family reunions if they could make it at all. They always felt they didn't see them enough and that always had bothered the family.

They were happy to see Ted and Kyle, welcomed Elaine with open arms and understood the circumstances and never judged or questioned. They were the best people one could ever want to meet and it thrilled Ted to think of them as family.

Even if they were family by marriage. They always accepted you for what and who you are and never pointed fingers or blamed. Ted was happy he had made the trip. He always felt like he was part of a family when he came here and this trip was no different.

The morning they left to start back to Iowa was one of sadness for all of them. It was tearing Ted apart and he wanted desperately to take her in his arms and tell her to get back in her car and follow them home. In his heart though he just knew that he couldn't do that.

He knew this was the best thing for her, for all of them for that matter. He once again had to love her enough to let go and let go he did, once more. He thought he should be used to it by now, but he wasn't and probably never would be.

The trip back only took him and Kyle a day and soon they were knee deep in work and bids again. Mandy took the job at the school and Tommy called and said they would be home for good in three weeks. It was sad times to shut some doors and happy times to open others. Ted just knew that this would all work out in the end.

He knew that they were all growing up, growing older and hopefully getting wiser. That's all we can really hope for in the end now isn't it? He thought to himself. He just knew they would all be fine. Elaine was starting a new life in a new area and Tommy would be home to begin a fresh as well. Life was good, as good as it could get anyway.

Chapter 15

Tommy and his family returned and soon settled back into the house that Tommy had called home his entire life. Of course Ted and Kyle took a small crew over and went through the house with a fine-toothed comb. They wanted everything just perfect when he came home, and it was.

The old house got a fresh coat of paint and anything that needed attention or replacing was done. Ted had new appliances installed as the ones left in the house were almost as old as Tommy. Everything that could be done was and it was soon ready. The house was in perfect shape for its new occupants.

Soon Tommy was fully hands on in the business and discovered rapidly that his dad and brother had quickly built a forerunner in the construction field. It was fast becoming the largest construction business in the area. Tommy was happy to be a part of it finally.

He had helped with some of the plans and design work from his duty station but never really felt like he was a part of it until now. He soon discovered that his dad had built a much bigger company than anything he ever imagined.

Business was booming and within a year something happened that Ted had only laughed off at the time as a joke. He was signing papers to buy his old boss out and take over his company. Ted never really gave it a second thought but now it was becoming a reality.

He looked back over the last two years and saw just how fast and large his little investment had become. It was mind boggling to say the least. He never in a million years would have believed that his little remodeling business would grow into this.

Their growth didn't stop with the acquisition of his old job either. Within six months they had bought several smaller companies out and were now the largest construction company in Iowa. Ted had only started the little company to occupy his free time and give him something to take his mind off Elaine. Now as he looks back over the last two and a half years he was stunned.

Along with the growth and success the business experienced came something else Ted had never thought he would have to consider. How to manage the money he suddenly had. After a visit with his accounting department it was discovered that Ted is a very wealthy man. He is rich and never even gave it a second thought.

He just knew that all the bills were paid and he didn't have to worry about disconnect notices in his mailbox anymore. He never gave being rich a second thought. As this was not his intent when he started the company. He just wanted something to do so he didn't dwell on his divorce.

He consulted a local financial planner he knew and trusted and soon had his finances in order. Of course with his success Mandy, Kyle and Tommy also had to consult this planner as well. They suddenly realized they too were extremely wealthy as well.

The tiny company their dad had started as nothing more than to consume time had suddenly become a giant in the field. Ted couldn't resist helping in any way he could and secretly arranged for a rather sizeable savings account in Elaine's name in Indiana.

He was pretty sure she could use the money and didn't want to see her have to break her back the rest of her life to get by. She had been a part of the company and was still family and always would be. He felt that he owed that much to her.

Elaine was of course taken back by his generosity but knew better than to question or refuse it. She could use the money and was grateful that he included her in the end result of his hard work and determination. She only wished he had given her another chance to show him that they could work as well.

Ted knew that the company was in good hands with Tommy and Kyle and started being less involved in the day to day operations of the business. He still was the boss, he just didn't go in every day and work ten hours a day like he used to.

He started spending more time in his flower gardens and with his grandchildren. Life had taken him on a roller coaster of a ride over the past few years and he was suddenly glad he could step back and relax a bit. He also liked the time he could now spend with the grandchildren. That was something he could never do too much of.

The kids were all fine and didn't have any worries anymore. Elaine seemed to be doing well from what he was told. He called her family in Indiana all the time and got updates on how she was doing. Of course he wouldn't hear of her knowing that he was watching over her, but he still was.

The grandchildren were all growing fast and he was finally at a point in his life where he felt content. He didn't really know if he could call it happiness or not, but he was content. And for now, that was just fine with him.

The company was continuing to grow and prosper and they suddenly found themselves doing more and more jobs out of state. The boys were doing a fine job governing the growth of the company and he couldn't have been prouder of them.

He may have planted the seed, but they cultivated it into the dream it was today. He was ecstatic that they had wanted to follow in this venture with him. After some serious discussion, they decided it was time to buy a company jet and hire a pilot.

The jobs were getting bigger and more complicated and the distance was becoming greater as well. They knew it made perfect sense after examining what they were spending on commercial air travel and what it would cost them to own their own aircraft.

It was agreed that it was the only logical step and soon he and the boys were shopping for a plane. If anyone had told him that he would be doing something like this four years ago he would have laughed at them. Yet here he was today shopping for a plane.

The family also agreed that a plane would give Elaine much better access to the family and her visits could become more frequent. He knew they all missed her and wanted to see more of her anytime they got the chance.

He thought it was a wonderful idea to offer her a way to spend weekends and holidays with them without her having to drive for ten hours to do it. Besides, after driving there and back it usually only left her a day or two to spend with the kids and grandchildren and that didn't quite seem like it was worth the effort.

Besides he was happy that he was now in a position to offer her such luxuries even if she was his ex. She was still the mother of his children and grandma to the grandchildren. She always would be and shouldn't feel like she is being punished because she chose to move.

He knew how much she missed them all and thought this would be a great way for her to spend more time with them and still lead her life in Indiana as well. It would be the best possible fit for all of them and Elaine couldn't have been happier.

Soon the holidays, birthdays and family gatherings had them all together again and they all loved it. Ted still hurt when he watched Elaine leave after every visit and just figured that he always would. He still loved Elaine even after all this time and decided he would probably never stop.

It didn't tear him up inside to see her leave like it used to, but it still hurt nonetheless. Tommy and Kyle built beautiful new homes on the outskirts of Council Bluffs and built Mandy and her family a new custom home on an acreage outside town as well. They just loved living in the country and the space it gave them.

They all nagged their dad constantly to let them build him a nice new home as well but Ted wouldn't leave his old white frame house for anything. He loved it now as much as he did that first day he pulled up in front of it. He wouldn't trade it for the largest mansion, although he could afford it.

All his friends and family were so pleased to see that success and money hadn't changed him one bit. He still drove his old pickup, lived in his little white frame house and still did his own shopping, cooking and cleaning. Money hadn't changed him a bit, he was still the same old Ted and they loved him for it.

The kids were always telling him to move and hire people to help him but he wouldn't hear of it. They loved their dad for the man he was not for the man he could be if he wanted to flaunt his money. They couldn't have been prouder of him. His big old yard was always full of kids from the neighborhood, grandchildren and family.

They still grilled out every weekend, weather permitting, and were the definition of family. Yes, Ted was at a point in his life where he could say that he was content and loved it. He still didn't know if he would ever meet anyone and try romance again, but he was content.

He loved to sit on his patio and dream of the day that Kyle, Tommy and Mandy's boys might step into the business and work side by side with their dads. He only hoped they would develop the love for building things their dads had developed and would want to carry the business into the future.

He knew it would be in good hands if they did. It was times like this that Ted suddenly realized the emptiness and sorrow he felt just a few years ago was nearly gone. He can still remember those feelings as though it was yesterday. But now they are but a distant memory.

His children were growing up and becoming successful. His family was together and growing stronger with each day and even Elaine seemed to finally be at peace and happy where she was. It was finally time to put the hurt and emptiness away once and for all and just be happy with the way his life was going.

He still wasn't overly joyed at the thought of spending it alone, but if that is what he had to do, it would be just fine. He would be just fine. He had come a long way in these past few years. He had grown a lot as a person, a dad and grandfather. He has developed into a person he likes.

That was something he wasn't sure he could do after their breakup. Become a person he would be able to like again. He had overcome some large obstacles to get to this point but he had done it. He was a better person for it too.

He chose to learn from the mistakes and not make them again. Maybe that seems to be why he always finds a reason to not date seriously again. Maybe he just feels that he is better off as he is and doesn't want to take the chances involved.

He still goes out on dates, not nightly, but he does go out. He enjoys the ladies company that he goes out with. He just seems to be unable to allow them into his life to any degree of seriousness. He thinks of them as merely good friends he is spending time with instead of a love interest.

He isn't even sure if he could allow himself to love again. Maybe what Elaine did made him unable or unwilling to ever love or trust again. After all, Elaine had wanted another chance with him and he was smart enough to say no to even her.

Whatever the reason or reasons, he was content to keep things as they were and not rock the boat, so to speak. His life seems to be on track again and it's a full life. He has everything he could possibly want, or does he?

He still thinks from time to time how great it would be to have someone to spend the rest of his life with. Then the moment passes and he chalks it up as a bad idea and leaves it alone. Why mess with things when they seem to be working out as well as they are?

It isn't like he has women beating a path to his door because he was named the most eligible bachelor in town or anything. Then again, he has managed to keep his success and wealth low key too. It isn't like he is taking out full page ads in the local paper saying "I'm rich and available" either.

He has managed to keep his newfound wealth pretty much a secret and likes it like that. He knows there are women out there that would jump at the chance to land a wealthy husband. He would rather be wanted for the man he is, not the size of his bank account.

Maybe he realizes this and that's the reason he isn't letting anyone get too close or taking anything too seriously right now. He is afraid that someone might only want his money and not him. At least Elaine wanted him for the man he was. Not for what he had or didn't have. Of course there was that problem with her cheating on him too though. He was content with his life and it was going to stay that way. He had no intentions on changing anything.

Chapter 16

It was a picture perfect autumn day in Iowa. The mornings still brisk and cool and the afternoons hot and unforgiving. The leaves were starting to change color and soon they would be full of brilliant hues of orange and red. Ted had always loved this time of year.

Today he was lazily strolling up and down aisles of the supermarket. Chips and dip, summer sausage, lots of soda and plenty of supplies for burgers and hot dogs on the grill placed in the cart. Yes today he was shopping for "Football Sunday" with his boys.

They both would be over soon to watch football on television with him, something they had done since they were kids. They never seemed to miss a game. Today the house and yard would be full and the TV would be blaring.

As he rounded the end of one aisle and stared to turn down the next he was wakened from his daze by a sudden jerk and crash. "What in the world?" he asked himself as he focused on the present. "I'm so terribly sorry" was all he heard from the woman bending over picking up items that had been knocked from his cart.

"I don't know what in the world I was thinking about" she continued and apologized over and over. Ted assured her that it was fine as he wasn't really paying attention either and the crash was probably inevitable.

As he took a good look at the woman standing before him now he was taken back. He knew her from somewhere, but where he thought. She looked at him with the most peculiar look on her face. It was as if she knew him too but couldn't place from where. Suddenly as if coached they both said "it's you."

Here in front of him was a woman he hadn't seen in ages or thought about for eons. She was a girl that he grew up with in his old neighborhood with his parents. Her parents lived a couple of doors down from them and she was always coming around trying to hang out with him.

She was of course a few years younger than him and he had only thought of her as a nuisance. She of course had the biggest crush on him and thought he was her first love. He didn't know that she even existed for the most part. He was not interested and thought of her as just the little kid down the street.

"Sandy, is that you?" he managed to get out. She confirmed it was her and told him how good it was to see him after all these years. They quickly found their way to the café located in the market to sit and catch up on old times.

She was the kid from down the street that he really never wanted around. This is until he got into high school and she started junior high. She suddenly became more than the little pain from down the street. She was fast becoming a real beauty and she thought the world of him. She hadn't changed a bit and was still easy on the eyes.

She was barely more than five feet tall and very petite built. She had long auburn hair that hung to her butt and the most beautiful brown eyes he could ever remember. Even back then she had a very full bust for a small girl and a body that would make men melt.

He actually got up the nerve to ask her out a few times and they dated on and off throughout his high school years. She was in love and he thought he might be to. Back then they both just knew that they were destined to be together forever. Of course that was before Elaine came along and stole his heart.

Sandy really never did forgive her for that, or him for letting her for that matter. She always thought they would marry, have children and live into their nineties. Funny how much things change from high school to today.

He saw her once in a while after high school when he went to visit him parents. They even dated again briefly as he and Elaine did break up a time or two during the early days. He lost track of her though when he learned that Elaine was pregnant and the rest as they say, is history.

He hadn't thought about this woman in years and here she was. He had always thought she moved away and hated him for not choosing her over Elaine. He was finding out now that she, like him, had lived here in town all her life. As he looked back now, he wasn't sure that he had made the right choice by picking Elaine.

She never did move away, just moved on with her life. She married but never had children and even lived in her parents old house for a while. After they both passed on. Ted's parents both had passed as well and he never gave it a thought to see if she might still be in the old neighborhood while he was cleaning out their house and getting it ready to sell. Had he just taken a few moments to walk down a couple of doors he would have found her still there.

They talked and caught each other up on everything from his divorce to the present. He found out that she too was divorced after her husband had left her. "Another woman?" he asked. She burst out in an almost hysterical laugh. "I'm sorry" she said. "It still makes me laugh when I think back" she went on.

Seems her husband left her for another all right. Another man. He spit his coffee all over the floor. "You've got to be kidding right?" he had to ask. "I wish I was" she told him and they both laughed until they thought they would cry.

Before leaving he discovered that she lived in an apartment not far from the little house he lives in now. He couldn't believe that they had lived that close and never ran into each other until today. She told him that she did exactly what he did for a very long time. Shut out the world and felt sorry for herself.

She blamed herself for everything and pretty much closed herself off to the world around her. Only allowing her closest friends to get close to her. Ted told her he knew exactly what that felt like.

Before leaving he decided to ask if she might like to drop by the house later for their little football frenzy and enjoy a burger on the grill. She said she would love to and got his address. After saying their goodbyes they each headed off in different directions. He was glad he had ran into her today. Well to be exact, she had run into him today. Literally.

As he pulled into the drive he saw that Tommy and Kyle and their families were already there. Mandy would be the last to arrive. She always was. He always told her that she was going to be late for her own funeral. She told her dad that as long as she wasn't late for his, it didn't matter. The boys came out and helped carry groceries in the house. Actually they just wanted the chips and dip and thought the only way they would get it was to help. He had to smile because deep down, he knew that they were right.

As they unpacked and put the items away he told them about his little accident at the supermarket. They couldn't believe that it happened to be someone he had grown up with and lost track of. He told them about inviting her to join them and they both nearly jumped. "Now we can get some dirt on you from when you were a kid" Tommy smirked.

Kyle just gave him a high five and said "yeah." He told them both to calm down as this woman really wasn't around him enough to give them any dirt on him. This burst their bubble quickly. They still had hope that she could tell them something.

The grill was just being warmed up and everyone was picking the best vantage point to watch TV from as Sandy arrived. Ted quickly went through the introductions and told her to make herself comfortable.

Of course the boys pulled her aside asking for any dirt on their dad as a young man anyway. They were quickly told that she really couldn't help them that much as she didn't actually hang around with their dad when she was younger.

She explained that she was younger and he was one of the popular kids that everyone wanted to hang out with. She told them that she was considered to be more a pain in the butt than anything else by their dad. They huddled in a corner and hung on her every word.

She of course wasn't much help in dishing up any dirt but she was helpful in letting them have a glimpse of what their dad was like when he was younger. Ted was glad he had asked her to join them. Even though she might be spilling some well kept secrets.

The game was a nail-biter and kept them all on the edge of their seats the entire time. The food was great as usual and everyone just loved Sandy and her company. Ted was glad she had nearly ran him over in the market now. He had often wondered what had happened to her and what she might be doing. He just hadn't realized how much till now. She had always been one of those friends he knew he could count on no matter what. She was always there for him.

It's so sad that we all seem to lose track of some of our closest friends like that as we grow older. He was glad this friend had found her way back into his life. He had always been able to talk to her about anything and suddenly realized how much he missed that.

Maybe she could give him a woman's perspective on what had happened between him and Elaine. Maybe it would make more sense if he heard it from her point of view. He was just glad he had ran into her and happier that she had accepted his invitation to join them today.

As the evening wound down Sandy dove right in and helped clear dishes and put things away. The kids all enjoyed her company almost as much as Ted had and he was glad they took to her so quickly.

She really had been a good friend as he was growing up. Even if he went out of his way to treat her like he wasn't aware that she existed. Before he knew it the kids and grandchildren were all saying their goodbyes and I love you's before leaving for their own homes.

They all made it a point to tell Sandy how much they enjoyed meeting her. They said they hoped she wouldn't be a stranger now that she knew where their dad lived. She assured them that they would be seeing a lot of her in the future.

She stayed to make sure Ted didn't need any help putting anything away before saying her goodnight as well. Ted told her to stop by anytime as he was usually there and she assured him she would. He walked her to the door and said he was glad they ran into each other and looked forward to future visits.

He watched until she was safe and in her car and pulling away before closing the door. He couldn't get over running into her after all these years. She had woven her way in and out of his thoughts from time to time over the years. Mostly just him wondering where she might be and how she was. It's kind of funny how we lose track of childhood friends only to run into them unexpectedly somewhere. He turned off all the unnecessary lights and things and settled on the couch to watch some TV before calling it a night. As he flipped from channel to channel, he found his thoughts wandering back to his younger days. He had always wondered what might have happened had he and Elaine not gotten married.

Would he have ended up with Sandy or found someone else in the end? He had never told anyone before but had always liked Sandy. They even dated before he and Elaine got together. And, like any typical high school couple, he and Elaine had their moments and broke up and got back together several times.

It was during his on and off again times with Elaine that he and Sandy really seemed to get somewhat close. She was always there for him and he just kind of took it for granted now that he looks back on it all. He never considered himself one that would do something like that to someone but it was quite clear now that he had.

Now he was kind of amazed that Sandy spoke to him at all let alone accept his invitation to join them today. He suddenly felt terrible for how he had treated her as a kid. He was always being told by others in the neighborhood that she had the biggest crush on him. He just passed it off as he didn't see her as anything but a nuisance. That was until she got a little older and he really started to notice her.

Now that he reflects back, he can see it clearly. He was too busy doing anything that didn't include Sandy when he was younger and he knew now that it had to have hurt her. Finding nothing on TV that held his attention he decided to call it an evening and turn in. Tomorrow would be another day and another fresh start with the world. He had given his past enough thought for one day.

As he went around making sure he had locked the doors and turned everything off, something caught his eye. There on the kitchen counter was a piece of paper folded up. He knew that it hadn't been there before, he would have noticed it. He unfolded the paper to find a note from Sandy inside. It just said that she had a wonderful time and was glad they had ran into each other. It also had her phone number on it and said to call anytime he needed someone to talk to.

Suddenly thoughts of Sandy were flooding his mind, she was all he could think about and it was a bit unnerving. Who would have thought that after all these years and everything that had happened to them both that he would think of her like this. She had been buried deep in his memories and didn't honestly think he would ever dig them up again. Until now.

He quickly put the note in his address book to keep it safe. He knew if he put it anywhere else, he would surely lose it. And right now, losing her number was the last thing he wanted to do. He almost picked up the phone and called her right then and there but thought better of it. He didn't after all want to seem desperate or anything. He did know one thing for sure though, he wanted to see her again, and soon.

He did a final check of the house before heading for his room. As he lay there staring at the ceiling, unable to sleep, Sandy kept sweeping through his mind like an unexpected Iowa storm. It came out of nowhere, no one saw it coming, but there it is. Full of fire and fury and had to be dealt with. He felt like a school kid again that was afraid to tell a girl he liked her. Mostly for fear she wouldn't like you and everyone would make fun of you for confessing your feelings in the first place.

He shook his head to clear the thoughts and tried again to get some sleep. He could deal with these thoughts some other time. Right now he just needed to clear his mind and drift slowly off to sleep. He just had to clear his mind....and he was out.

Chapter 17

Ted woke the next morning to birds chirping outside his window and a gentle autumn breeze blowing the blinds back and forth. He could see that the sun was up and it was going to be another hot fall day. He stretched and slowly got out of bed and headed to the kitchen to start a much needed pot of coffee.

As he reached for the coffee, his hand brushed his address book and he quickly opened it and looked at the note and number Sandy had left the night before. As coffee brewed, he picked up the phone and without even thinking dialed her number.

Before he could stop himself and hang up she answered. He told her good morning and asked if she had plans for lunch. She told him she didn't and they quickly agreed on meeting later at a restaurant nearby. He told her how good it had been to see her again and said they could do some more catching up at lunch. As he hung up the phone, he wondered why in the world he had just done that. It was as if someone else's hand had dialed that phone, but it was his.

He showered, shaved and made himself as presentable as he could before calling Kyle and Tommy at the office. He asked if they had anything pressing that needed his undivided attention and they assured him they had everything under control.

He told them he would have his cell phone on all day if they needed to reach him and finished dressing. Kyle asked what he was doing for dinner and told him that he was more than welcome to stop by the house later. It was chili night. He said he would be there and told his son goodbye.

He loved chili even though it didn't always agree with him. He was willing to pay the price of a little heartburn for some homemade chili. He quickly sat out the antacid as he knew that he would need it tonight.

Kyle's chili was hot and spicy and his heartburn would be four alarm tonight, he just knew it. As he went about his daily chores and readied himself for his lunch date, the phone rang. He fully expected it to be either Kyle saying that something had come up or Sandy backing out at the last minute. He was wrong on both counts.

It was Elaine on the other end. He was a bit taken back as she really didn't call unless it was important or something had happened. Her time in Indiana seemed to be agreeing with her and she called less and less lately.

They still saw her for important gatherings and holidays, but other than that, she didn't come to visit much lately. Of course he asked her if everything was all right immediately. She put his fears to rest by telling him she was fine and everything and everyone there were good.

She did tell him that she had something very important to talk to him about and asked if he could get a few days away and come down. He again asked if everything was ok and she quickly said yes. She just said that she had something important to talk to him about and wanted to do it in person.

He told her that he would make all the arrangements and be there by the end of the week. He could stay the whole weekend that way. She was delighted and said she would see him soon and hung up.

Now his mind was racing and his thoughts were going in a million places at once. He couldn't help but fear that something was wrong. He did something he wouldn't normally do. He would usually just take Elaine's word for it that everything was fine. Not this time, he quickly made a few calls to her family.

They all told him that everything was fine there and they were pretty sure they knew why she wanted him to come down. They also told him that it was Elaine's place to talk to him and not theirs. They did offer one bit of information that might have shed some light on what was going on though.

It appears that Elaine had been seeing a local man, a really nice guy, for some time now. They all thought that it might be getting serious and thought that maybe that is what she wanted to see him about. He of course swore them to secrecy and told them to keep his phone calls to themselves. They agreed wholeheartedly and said the calls never took place. He had one more call he just had to make before meeting Sandy for lunch.

He called the office and asked Kyle and Tommy if the plane would be needed the end of the week and weekend. They both said no and quickly asked him why. He told them of the call from their mom and she wanted to see him this weekend. They of course offered to go with him and he assured them it was fine.

"She just wants to talk to me in person about something and I feel that I owe her that" he told his boys. They agreed and said they would have the plan ready for him at the end of the week. He said he would leave Friday morning and return on Monday. They said to consider it done already.

He gathered a light jacket, his keys and cell phone before heading out the door. He looked at his watch as he started his truck and saw that he was already running late. He only hoped that Sandy wouldn't think that he had stood her up and leave.

As he pulled into the parking lot, he saw her car was still there. He breathed a sigh of relief as he didn't want her to think that he had blown her off or gotten cold feet at the last minute. He saw her at a nearby table as soon as he entered the eatery. He waved and walked directly to the table.

"I'm so sorry that I'm late" he told her as he pulled out a chair and sat down. "Not to worry Ted, I just figured that something came up and if you weren't here in an hour, I would have left and called later" she told him. He was so glad she was being this understanding about the whole thing.

But then again, it wasn't like this was a real date or anything. It was just two old friends meeting for lunch, right? He quickly dismissed his thoughts and explained that something in fact had came up at the last minute and he had to deal with it.

She said she totally understood and for him not to worry. She wasn't going to be that easy to get rid of this time. He wasn't really sure what she meant by that but decided not to give it another thought. They ordered lunch and soon became lost in conversation about the good old days. She filled him in on what had been happening in her life and told him she kind of knew a little of what had happened in his.

He learned that she was aware of the divorce and his accident. She told him that more than once she almost found herself at the hospital to see him. He told her that he really wished she had stopped. She was uncertain if her stopping would cause any problems with Elaine or not and thought better of the idea.

He assured her that he didn't think it would have caused any problems and wished she had came to visit anyway. As they talked and filled in all the blank spaces spanning nearly thirty years he learned some things he never knew before now.

It appears that Elaine went out of her way to confront Sandy just before they got married. Elaine had always known of Sandy's crush on him. Elaine made it a point to let Sandy know that she was pregnant and that her and Ted would be getting married and she needed to keep her distance. "I am so sorry Sandy, I had no idea she did anything like that to you" he told her. She said she knew he didn't know what Elaine had done.

"She wasn't a fool Ted, she knew we dated and knew that I would always be there to pick up the pieces should you two not work out" Sandy told him. "She was just trying to protect what she saw as hers and I understand that" she went on.

"As a matter of fact, had the tables been turned, I think I might have done the very same thing" she said. He still told her again how sorry he was that Elaine had done that. He didn't know she could be so hurtful and mean to another person like that. That was a side of her he never saw until their split.

Sandy of course said that was a long time ago but it was in the back of her mind and the main reason she never stopped while he was in the hospital. Now that he knew everything, he could understand her reasoning. He wasn't happy about Elaine doing that to her all those years ago, but he could at least understand now. He had just thought that she moved on and gotten over him. She just laughed and told him she didn't think she would ever truly be over him, then their meal arrived.

That comment completely took him by surprise, he thought she had forgotten all about him years ago. Only to learn today that she might still have some sort of feelings for him. Now that gave him food for thought.

They finished their meal with only small talk and some warm memories of the old neighborhood. After lunch Ted walked her to her car and told her he had a wonderful time and hoped to see her soon. She just said "you have my number" as she got in her car and waved as she pulled away.

The rest of the day was spent running errands and getting things together for his unplanned trip the end of the week. Dinner at Kyle's was as usual, fun filled with laughs and love. The chili was great and hot and only after goodbyes, hugs, kisses and I love you's were said did Kyle walk his dad to his truck.

He waved as Ted pulled away and watched till his dad was out of sight before going back into the house. As soon as Ted was in his truck and moving he dialed Sandy and said he hoped it wasn't too late. She assured him it wasn't and told him he could call anytime.

He asked her if she would like to have dinner with him the next evening. She happily accepted and asked where and what time. Ted told her that he would pick her up this time and would see her around six. They said their goodnights and he said he would see her tomorrow evening.

As he pulled into his drive, he couldn't help but notice that the last two days his mind had been filled with nothing but thoughts of Sandy. He wasn't quite sure right now just what those thoughts meant but knew it made him happier than he had been in a very long time to think about her. And he liked that.

He went in the house and decided that now was as good a time as any to pack and get ready for his upcoming trip. He took out a bag and packed things he knew he wouldn't need the rest of the week and only kept out medicine and toiletries that could be packed Friday morning before leaving.

He took some antacid before the nagging burn he was beginning to experience got out of control and stopped him from sleeping tonight. As he turned on the TV and flipped from one station to another he kept thinking about how much fun he had today with Sandy.

He hadn't let himself go and be that at ease with anyone in a very long time and it really felt good. Reflecting back he thought it funny how we all have roads we follow throughout life. Some find us on paths that we feel are meant to last us a lifetime. Others are full of twists and turns that drive us from the normal path all together. Only to lead us down new, strange and undiscovered paths. Some of those new roads lead us to new and exciting places while others leave us wishing we had turned back before it was too late.

He had taken a lot of roads and paths to get to where he was in his life today. Some had been full of surprises and some he wished he hadn't taken at all. Some had been filled with roadblocks and obstacles and others just wound up being dead-ends. He had always thought that no matter what, he would always walk those paths and roads with Elaine.

Always thought they would explore and discover both the pleasures and pitfalls of those new and undiscovered roads together. Now here he seemed to be at yet another crossroad in those paths through life. Which road should he take this time he wondered?

He still didn't think it was too late to change things and ask Elaine back into his life. He could try to patch some of those holes in the roads they took and see if they couldn't finish out this life together on the same path.

Another path seemed to lead him toward leaving things as they are and just being content to be alone. And here was a new, undiscovered path that was looming on the horizon. It was one he wasn't sure yet that he could see clearly but it was one that he knew would once again be full of uncertainty.

The new path might lead him to discover something he passed by as a young man and never realized he missed. Maybe it was just a path that would lead him back to something and someone that was familiar to him. Maybe this new path was nothing but a circle and he finally made it back to the beginning, so he could start anew. The only thing he knew for certain at this moment was he had to face head on whatever it was that Elaine had to discuss with him first.

That road had to be either closed permanently or temporarily put under construction to fix what was wrong with it before he decided on any new roads and paths. If closing it forever is what was meant to be then he would be the first to put up the "road closed" signs.

He just knew that this time he had to see Elaine with an open mind. He couldn't go see her with any expectations or bitterness of the past haunting him. It had to be done without any of their baggage from the past weighing either of them down. He would see where this road would lead the end of the week.

For now he had to be content with things the way they were. He couldn't afford to jump to conclusion when it came to Elaine. He had learned that the hard way from their past. If she merely wanted his blessing to move on and start fresh with someone new as her family believed was the case, he had to be happy for her and walk away once and for all. If she wanted to ask one last time if there might be any kind of chance of them getting back together and working things out, he would have to look at that as well.

If she was only seeking his blessing and approval to be happy with someone else, he had to be prepared to give her both. Whatever became of his trip this weekend he knew one thing for certain. It had to either be put to rest once and for all or resurrected and revived.

Either way, it would have to be final once and for all when he returned next week. No looking back, no second guessing, just final. He finished packing and took his bags into the living room and sat them by the door.

Now all he needed to do was get over this overwhelming urge to pick up the phone and call Sandy and ask if he could come over. He couldn't explain why but he just had the urge to see her. This was unlike anything he had experienced in years. He suddenly found that waiting till tomorrow evening to see Sandy wasn't something he wanted to do. He wanted to see her now and hadn't had feelings like this for anyone since junior high.

We all had the major love of our lives early in junior high. The one we couldn't go without seeing each and every day. He was suddenly feeling just like that and couldn't explain why. It was ludicrous he thought to himself.

He isn't in junior high and he sure isn't a kid anymore and shouldn't be feeling like this as a responsible adult. It was so unlike him. He was the cool, calm and collected type that everyone always turned to. Here he was acting like a lovesick puppy and didn't know why.

Before he could pull himself back to reality, he was already dialing the phone. The words escaping his lips were surely not his own he thought as he asked Sandy if he could come over. She told him that he was welcome to stop by any time he wanted. He could only say that he would be there shortly. As he drove to Sandy's apartment he couldn't believe he was doing it or what in the world he would say when he got there. "This is crazy" he mumbled as he drove along.

As she opened the door, the only thing he could think of was to tell her he needed someone to talk to. She told him that she offered to listen anytime he found the need for someone to talk to.

He was never one that was good on his feet, so to speak, and could only think of telling her about Elaine's call earlier that day. He told her that he thinks he found out why she wants him to come down and they talked into the night. He suddenly was so glad that he had found her because she was always one that he found it easy to talk to.

He had always been able to tell Sandy everything and soon found that he still could. He told her every little detail about their breakup and filled her in on everything that had happened since. She didn't judge or make snide comments, she just listened.

He found is felt good to have someone that would just listen. He hadn't really had anyone that he felt he could turn to before now. She would be the first person to really know everything and he was finally getting to tell his side of all this. Even if it was years after the fact, it still felt good to unburden himself from all this.

He had kept all this bottled up inside himself for years and thought until now that he was over it. Until now he just thought that he would never find anyone that would just listen and let him tell his side of all this mess. It felt good to finally unlock all this that he had kept buried deep inside himself for so long.

It felt right to tell this all to Sandy, a person he had all but forgotten about from his past. She seemed to honestly understand how he felt and what he had gone through. Maybe in a way, she did he thought.

After all, she too had been married and found her spouse cheating on her. Her situation was different yet somehow very similar. She knew what it felt like to be betrayed and lied to. She knew the sheer agony of going through a breakup.

She knew what it felt like to have to start over and make a new life for herself. She knew probably better than anyone he could think of how he felt. Talking to her now like this was suddenly the best idea he had ever had he thought.

They talked until they could both barely keep their eyes open and Ted decided that it was past time to go home. He thanked her for listening and told her to get some sleep. He asked if their dinner plans were still on and she quickly told him they were. She hugged him and kissed his cheek ever so lightly. She told him to call anytime and that she would see him later that evening. He again thanked her and headed for his truck.

This time he went home feeling more at ease than he could remember in a very long time. He had no trouble falling asleep as soon as his head was on his pillow. Tonight would be one of the first nights he would sleep peacefully in a very long time.

__Chapter 18__

Ted heard the honking of a horn and knew that it was Kyle there to pick him up and take him to the plane. He quickly grabbed his bags and headed for the door. Just as he opened the door Kyle was reaching for the doorknob. "About time you got ready, you're worse than an old woman" he jokingly told his dad as he reached out and took his bags. "I could find something else to do to be even longer if you would like" he told his son and laughed. "If you take any longer, you're walking to the airport" Kyle told him.

As they drove along, Kyle asked again if his dad wanted him to go with him. "It isn't too late for me to pack a bag and come with you dad" Kyle told him. Ted told him that he would be fine and that he would be back Monday. Kyle waited until his dad was safely seated and ready for takeoff before he left.

Soon he was on his way and would be there in just over an hour and a half. It amazed him that they could travel over six hundred miles in such a short time. He was just glad that he wasn't driving it. That would be an all day drive and he did not want that.

Soon they were landing and his rental car was waiting at the terminal for him. He quickly arrived at her aunt's house and was immediately met by waves and hugs. He always had enjoyed the visits they had here. Elaine wasn't home from work yet but he was quickly whisked inside for something to drink.

Her aunt would not take no for an answer. He wasn't about to argue with her either, he knew she would win. They laughed and talked and she told him that she had read about his company in the newspaper.

They were amazed and so very proud of him and the success he had achieved. They couldn't have been prouder of him if he had been relation by blood instead of marriage. Before he knew it time had passed and Elaine was walking through the door. She quickly came over and hugged him and thanked him for coming like this. He told her it wasn't a problem and she knew he would come anytime she needed him to. She said she knew but still appreciated it.

After she showered and changed they decided to go to one of their favorite old restaurants and talk. He still wasn't sure why she had asked him here but hoped he soon would. They were seated quickly and ordered their meal.

As they waited for their meal to arrive, Elaine started by telling him that she was so very sorry for everything she had put him through these last few years. He told her not to worry about it and said that she hadn't asked him to come all this way just to apologize.

She told him he was right and told him that she had met someone and it was becoming serious. It was as her family had suspected and really came as no shock to him. Deep down he knew she wasn't going to ask for one more chance. If that were the case, he knew she would have made the trip to him. She knew that their company jet was at her disposal anytime she needed it or wanted it. He put on his bravest face and told her how happy he was for her.

She told him that she wanted him to hear it directly from her and not get the news second or third hand. She told him that she honestly thought this man might ask her to marry him. He again told her that he was happy for her and wished her only the best. She said she did have a huge favor to ask this time and was hoping he would help her with it. He of course told her that he would do anything he could, all she had to do was ask.

She told him that it would really mean the world to her if the kids and grandchildren would be there this time. She told him that she really could understand them not wanting to be there when she married the man that broke up their marriage.

She couldn't at the time, but she can now that she opens her eyes and thinks about it. She of course extended an invitation for him to come as well but said she would understand if he couldn't.

"Having my children and grandchildren here with me would mean so very much to me this time Ted, will you help me?" she asked. He assured her that he would do everything in his power to get them all there when the time came. All she had to do was give him a date and time. She told him that she knew it was one of his famous talks that changed their minds about letting her back in their lives right after they split. "You knew about that?" he asked.

She told him that all three of the kids had pulled her aside and told her that had it not been for him, they would not have changed their minds. "They all made sure I knew that it was you that allowed me back into their lives" she told him.

It had never been his intention of her finding out that he had orchestrated all of that. She told him that she knew he was much too proud to admit it so she never brought it up. "If it hadn't been for you, I might still be on the outside looking in" she told him.

They talked through dinner and spent that whole weekend visiting old familiar places they always visited whenever they came here as a family. He was so very happy to see everyone and seeing all the old places they went to on every visit made the trip complete.

As he loaded his bags into the car for his trip back to the airport, she did ask two last things. "Can you ever find it in your heart to really forgive me Ted?" she asked for one. He assured her that he already had and would love her till he stopped drawing breath even if it meant living apart and separate lives.

The last thing she asked of him was to give it some serious thought to coming down if they set a date for a wedding. Any other time he would have told her no without hesitation. This time was somehow different. He told her that he would be honored to come this time and was sure the entire family would be there as well.

He left there that day with a little more than he came with. He left with closure once and for all. No more wondering if she would ask to come back and wondering if he would give in and let her. No more putting his life on hold for reasons he couldn't explain.

It was clear now that it was time to move on with his own life. He told her to call and let him know when she knew all the details and they would be there front and center. She kissed his cheek and told thanks and said she loved him.

He knew that it was more like the love one has for a best friend than anything and he returned the sentiment. They had been bitter and cold to each other long enough and it was finally time to move on once and for all. He was more than a little sad by all this. Deep down in his heart he was hoping she might ask for another chance.

In a way though, he was glad she hadn't. He knew that at this point in his life he would have said yes if she had. To be honest though, he also knew that would have been a terrible mistake. He was glad it ended like it did and only wished her the best.

Kyle met him at the airport and asked if everything was ok. He told him what had happened as they drove to his house. Kyle of course asked his dad if he was ok with all this. He assured Kyle that he was and told him of her request that they all come down if she marries this man. "What do you think dad, should we?" he asked. Ted was quick this time to tell his son that he thought it would be a great idea for all of them to attend this one.

It was as if a giant weight had been lifted off Ted and he was suddenly willing to accept peace. Elaine would be happy and he honestly believed that she would make an honest go of it this time. He had been assured that the man she was seeing was great. For the first time in a very long time he was happy for her. Truly happy this time. She deserved to be happy and he would do anything he could to see she got it.

After Kyle dropped him off, he unpacked and called Sandy. It was good to hear her voice and he asked if she was free for dinner tonight. She told him she was and would love to have dinner with him. He spent the rest of the day catching up on phone calls reading mail and piddling around the house.

It just felt good to be home and he wanted to do nothing in particular. That evening he got ready for dinner and drove over to pick Sandy up. She met him at the door with a big hug and asked if he was ok. He told her what had happened on his trip and she fully expected him to be crushed.

She was happily surprised to see how well he was handling all this and wasn't sure she could do it. They talked about the favors she asked of him and he told her he had every intention of fulfilling them if he could. She had never seen him like this and was glad to get to know the man the boy she knew had grown into. She was proud to call him friend and was silently hoping that friendship might blossom into more, much more.

She had decided to keep her feelings to herself while he was gone. She thought it best right now not to say anything. She didn't want him getting the wrong impression or feeling obligated to her in any way. He didn't owe her a thing. What had or hadn't happened between them as kids was well in the past. Besides, she wasn't sure those feelings were strong enough or true enough to build any kind of relationship on in the first place.

If anything at all were going to develop between them she wanted it to be because they worked for it. They went to dinner and caught a movie afterward as Ted said he really wasn't ready to call it an evening just yet. She agreed as she really didn't want to be without his company as well. They had a few laughs and a good evening but he seemed a bit distant after his trip. She was sure he had a lot on his mind and didn't want to pry.

They said their goodnights and Ted asked if he could call her again tomorrow. She told him to call anytime he wanted, kissed his cheek and told him goodnight. He left that night although he wanted nothing more than to ask her if he could stay. He also knew that tonight he should be alone to sort out his thoughts and feelings and put the past in the past where it belonged. He knew that once he dealt with all this on his own terms he would be much better prepared to look long and hard at what might be happening between him and Sandy.

He knew that he didn't want a repeat of the past. He wanted a fresh start and didn't want ghosts from the past haunting either of them. If anything was to develop between the two of them, it would have every chance of working. He went home that night and put the past behind him once and for all. It was a painful ending but an exciting and fresh start as well. He just knew that it was time to put up those road closed signs and move on.

He tossed and turned and didn't sleep well that night. Those old ghosts didn't give up easily but they were finally put to rest. He got up that morning feeling drained but alive for the first time in a long time. He put on coffee, showered and dressed and just sat and stared out the window. It was time to move on he decided and Sandy was the right path to take this time. He just felt it in his heart.

He had passed her by once upon a time and Ted was a smart enough man to know that very few of us get a second chance like this. He was also a smart enough man to know that if he didn't take this chance, he would regret it the rest of his life.

On more than one occasion he remembers thinking about "what if" he had stayed with Sandy. Specially during the early years and usually after he and Elaine had just had an argument. He must have pushed those thoughts out of his mind because he really hadn't even thought about them until now. Now they were as clear as if it had just happened yesterday. Maybe he had repressed those memories for years but he wasn't about to do it any longer.

It was that very moment that Ted decided he was going to take things slow and easy but would not let Sandy slip out of his life again without at least telling her how he felt. That happened once and it was not about to happen again. He did call Sandy later that day and told her that he was fine and asked if she might like to meet the next day for lunch. She of course jumped at the chance to see Ted again.

He spent the rest of the day closing out some things from the past that he felt needed to be done. He packed some old things he had found in their old house before Tommy moved in and sent them to Elaine.

He felt that it was time to let go. He called the boys, asked if he was needed for anything and just stayed around home for the entire day. He did spend a little time in his flower gardens and soon the yard looked spotless.

He ate alone that night, watched some TV and turned in early that evening. He felt drained yet he felt relieved and free for the first time

For Better, For Worse?

since he and Elaine had split up. Soon he had trouble staying awake and knew that it was time to turn in. He might just get a decent nights sleep tonight he thought as he checked the house one last time. After he was satisfied that everything had been put away, turned off and locked, he headed for his room.

That night his dreams were overflowing with images of Elaine, Sandy and everything that had happened over the last few years. It was as if he was purging all of this from his system through his dreams. Some were good, some were bad and some he couldn't recall at all. He did however get a good nights rest and woke feeling like he was ready to face the day. That was something he hadn't done in a long time. Most days he could care less if he even got out of bed.

As usual he started a pot of coffee, showered and dressed and made his way back to the kitchen. Today though instead of wallowing in the past and blaming himself for things that were beyond his control he found the phone book and opened it. He soon found the number of the florist he and Elaine had always used and called.

He ordered two dozen roses that day. One dozen white roses would be delivered to Elaine in Indiana with a card that simply read, "I will love you always, I wish you only the best and hope things work the way you want them to." "Let us know when the date is set and we will all be there in the front row cheering you on....Love Ted."

The second dozen were the most beautiful red roses the florist had and those were sent to Sandy. The card with those said, "we took separate roads years ago and although our paths winded and crossed we never seemed to find the path that led us back to each other." "We have finally found that path and I would like to explore it together....Ted." He knew it might sound a little cheesy but he couldn't help himself. He wanted Sandy to know that he didn't intend to let her get away again. Not this time.

Page 125

Chapter 19

The time passed quickly and soon another year had gone by. It was a year full of surprises and things happening on all fronts. The business absorbed several smaller companies and was growing beyond any of their dreams. With the growth came more jobs, more employees, more responsibilities and of course more money.

Ted couldn't believe that the little company he had started a few years ago was now one of the largest in the entire Midwest. It was a bit mind boggling to say the least. While he could take most of the credit for the concept, it was Tommy and Kyle that did the real work to develop and grow the company into what it is today.

Elaine did in fact get married to her new love Jerry. And as promised, Ted, the kids, and all the grandchildren were there front and center and couldn't be happier for her. Ted had done some detective work and found that although the man she was marrying was the nicest guy you could ever hope for, he and Elaine did struggle a bit to make ends meet.

He and the kids decided their wedding gift would be one they all knew Elaine could use. Ted and the kids pulled Elaine and Jerry aside and gave them an envelope. Inside was a very large check and they both were taken completely by surprise.

Ted had learned from her family that they both worked hard but had some bills that plagued them a bit and they were trying desperately to pay them off in order to give them both a fresh start.

It was a unanimous decision that she was still family and they now had enough money from the business that Ted's great, great, great grandchildren would be set for life. The check was more than enough to allow them to pay off all their bills, buy new vehicles, build a new home and have a nice nest egg for retirement.

They didn't know what to say when they opened it and Ted and the kids just hugged them both and told them to enjoy it. The entire day was perfect and everyone was happy to see the kids and how fast the grandchildren were growing up.

Elaine pulled Ted aside and told him how thankful she was that he and the kids came. She said that she now could understand why none of them were at her last wedding but happy they attended this one. She kissed his cheek and with tears in her eyes told him she loved him now and always. He cried that day too but for once they were tears of joy.

He really was happy for her and glad to see that she finally found the one she could settle down with. She hadn't had an easy time of it after their divorce either and he was just glad that she was finally happy. Ted even took Sandy with him and Elaine was shocked when she saw her.

Shocked that they had found each other after all these years. She did approach Sandy and apologize for the way she had treated her as a kid. She told Sandy that she was sorry for being a snotty high school drama queen and for acting like she did toward her.

Those were words Sandy really never thought she would hear from this woman but accepted them with grace and class. The rest of the trip was a good one and Sandy got to meet the rest of the family.

They all went to their favorite spots and visited as many places as they could before boarding their plane to return home again. This time they were leaving with a sort of finality to it. They all knew that Ted and the kids would still visit from time to time but also knew it would never be the same again.

The last year Ted and Sandy had been inseparable. They did everything together and Mandy, Kyle and Tommy were so happy for their dad. It looked like he had finally found some happiness of his own. If anyone deserved it, they knew that he did.

Ted and Sandy grew stronger and closer with each passing day and soon she was thought of as family. The kids all loved her to death and the grandchildren even called her grandma. Ted finally battled all his demons from the past and had won. He was happy and life was full for him again.

That was something he never thought he would experience again after he and Elaine divorced. Maybe all those failed dates were trials and tribulations to bring him full circle and back to Sandy. All he knew was he was happy with her in his life and wasn't about to ever let her get away again.

Yes, the grandchildren were growing up fast, the kids were all thriving and their lives were on track and Ted was happy. He just didn't think it could get any better than this.

He finally found peace in his and Elaine's breakup and could look back now not with bitterness and hate, but with a sense of growth and reason for it. It had been a time for him to grow as a person and find his own way in life.

The roads and paths had been many and full of heartbreak but he finally felt that he was on the right road now. He was all but retired from the business and Tommy and Kyle were doing an excellent job of running things. He knew it was in good hands and the only end in sight would be of their choosing, no one else's.

He finally got up the nerve to tell Sandy that he loved her and wanted her to be a very big part of his life. That was something he couldn't see himself doing just a few short years ago. She confessed that she had always loved him and would be happy to be a part of his life in whatever capacity he allowed her to be.

She was just glad they had found each other again after all this time and wasn't about to let him get away again either. He hadn't gone as far as to ask her to marry him, yet, but every one of his children had bets that he would.

Yes it had been a very full and surprising year and one they could all look back on and smile about. The hard times, hard feelings and sorrow seemed to have disappeared completely. This family in one way or another had paid their dues and now it was time to reap some of the rewards of their hard work. It had been a good year and one they could look back on with pride.

Mandy took over the job of principal at her school and loved her work immensely. Ted always knew she would go far and always told her that someday he would be calling her Superintendent. She of course told him that he was dreaming but secretly hoped her dad was right. Tommy, Kyle and Mandy's husband Dan had developed the business into one that was now doing work on a national level and they were doing a marvelous job of it.

Ted would never have believed that the little company he started to make some extra money would make him rich beyond belief someday. It had not only grown beyond his wildest dreams but had a reputation known all over the country as being not only one of the biggest, but the best.

He was so proud of the work they had done to get to this point. He couldn't have done it without his sons and he knew it. They deserved a lot of the credit for the company it had became today. He was always the first to tell them that too.

He and Sandy spent nearly every minute together and the kids couldn't figure out why their dad hadn't at least asked her to move in with him. Maybe it was just the values and morals he and Sandy had been raised by that stopped them from doing it. They were always together yet kept separate homes.

It didn't make any sense to them to see them live apart like that. They just figured in time they would take that last step and be together when they were ready. They just knew that they loved her as much as their dad did and would welcome her into the family with open arms.

Sandy never did have children of her own and at times felt that she had missed out on something in life. Specially when she saw how Ted and his children got along. She couldn't love his kids anymore if she had given birth to them herself and it was plain to see the feelings were mutual.

She knew that she would never replace their mom in their hearts or lives and didn't want to. Elaine would always be their mother and Sandy was smart enough to know this. She could only hope that they would accept her as an alternate mom if things worked out between her and Ted.

She didn't really have any doubts that it wouldn't work out as things were only getting better between them with each passing day.

As they grew closer, it was plain to see that Ted was allowing himself to love again. Sandy never doubted him when he told her that he loved her. She just knew that it had to be hard for him to give his heart fully to her after what he had been through with Elaine. She felt the same to an extent as she remembers how hurt and betrayed she felt when her own marriage fell apart.

Even though the circumstances were as different as day and night, the similarities were there as well. It was hard for her to not put up her guard when Ted said he loved her or when she told him she felt the same way. There was always going to be a bit of uncertainty deep down inside from what they both had been through in the past. That was only human nature and she knew it.

The time they spent together was getting to be more and more frequent and the time they spent apart was becoming less and less. She would have jumped at the chance to take this to a more permanent level had Ted asked her to move in with him.

That had not happened yet but she was still hoping it would soon. She knew that an adjustment like that would take time for both of them as they both had lived alone for some time now. And, a change like that would be a giant step for both of them. She knew it would take some getting used to but was willing to try if he ever asked her.

Ted too knew that it made no sense for them to maintain separate households. It was costing Sandy money to live in her apartment and he had plenty of room for her at his house. He suspected that she would say yes if he asked her to move in, he just wasn't sure he could just yet.

He loved her and knew this was real love, he just wasn't sure that moving in was the next logical step. He also didn't want to take too much time and drive her away from waiting. Although Ted didn't honestly think she would give up that easily he also didn't want to push it and find out.

For the most part he was very certain that Sandy would accept if he asked her to move in. He just wasn't completely certain that he was ready to take that step. In his heart it felt right but in the back of his mind something kept telling him to slow down and take his time.

The last thing he would want is for the two of them not to work out. And, he would never forgive himself if he discovered that his being too pushy or moving too fast was the cause of that to happen. He felt that he had just found her again and wanted everything to be just perfect for them when they took a more lasting move such as this.

He wanted nothing to chance when it came to giving them the much needed and deserved opportunity of making an honest to goodness go of things. They both had waited long enough and been through more than their share of disappointments as it was. At this point in their relationship he would do anything to guarantee success for the both of them.

He felt his world was complete when he was near her and couldn't imagine life without her when they were apart. He knew in the deepest recesses of his heart that this was a love that would last. She was the first thing he thought about in the morning and the last thing he could remember before closing his eyes at night. It was becoming clear to everyone around him that Sandy was fast becoming the very center of his entire world.

Sandy of course felt the same and only felt whole when she was beside him. Emptiness overtook her each night before she closed her eyes for sleep and it was driving her mad. Suddenly she couldn't imagine what her world would be like without Ted in it. They seemed to be the answer to each others prayers and everyone that knew them was rooting for them to make it.

When they were together people stopped and watched and just knew this was a couple in love. It was as if together they exuded a glow that could have lit up the entire universe. It was a light that could not be extinguished and would never fade. It was a love that most of us only wish we could find and even fewer know exist.

The saddest part of the whole situation was they seemed to be the only ones that couldn't see it. It was as if their troubled pasts were clouding their ability to entirely open up to one another and totally commit to each other. They just seemed to have trouble making that one final step that would seal their future for eternity.

Of course Ted's children did everything they could think of to drop subtle hints to them that they should just jump in with both feet and swim like crazy. Kyle and Tommy were ready to duct tape Ted to a chair until he came to his senses and Mandy was ready to lock Sandy in her room until she saw the light. They just hoped it didn't come to such measures.

Although, Tommy and Kyle assured Mandy that if that's what it would take they were more than game to try it. They all had a good laugh and decided to just stand by patiently and let them work it out on their own. They were all sure that they would finally get it right and things would work out for them. Tommy and Kyle still said they had the duct tape ready for plan B should they need it.

Chapter 20

Months passed and each day brought Ted and Sandy closer and closer. It was evident to all that knew them they were made for each other and would be happy the rest of their lives. Ted knew that it was time to take some steps he had been afraid to take until now. Suddenly he seemed to change almost overnight. No one could figure out just why though.

What they didn't know was Ted had made a phone call to Elaine and after more than an hour on the phone, he was ready to move on completely. Elaine told him that it was time he allowed himself the luxury of being happy. She told him that if anyone she ever knew deserved it, he did. It seemed that he would only allow himself to move on if he got her blessing and she gave it wholeheartedly.

Sandy was caught off guard and taken totally by surprise when Ted showed up at her apartment with boxes in his hand and asked if he could help her pack. She nearly knocked him over as she jumped into his arms and hugged him so tightly he thought he would pass out. Of course she said yes when he formally asked her to move in with him.

Those were words she had been waiting months to hear and it didn't take her long to say yes when she did hear them. Ted had just made her the happiest woman that ever lived when he did. Soon Tommy, Kyle, Mandy and all their friends were bringing in empty boxes and carrying out full ones. In no time at all she was officially moved out of her lonely little apartment and moved into Ted's little white frame house.

The adjustment period they both had been fearing seemed to elude them. They fit together as though they had been together their entire lives. It was uncanny and everyone was so happy for them. They looked like an old married couple and the house seemed to be full of love and life for the first time since he had moved in all those years ago. Yes, Ted felt whole again finally and he only had Sandy to thank for that.

The rest of that year, birthdays and holidays were truly a family event and the house was more than full of love. The kids and grandchildren stopped by all the time and Ted and Sandy was the perfect host. Elaine and Jerry joined them for most events and the family really seemed to be family again. It had taken all of them a lot of time and hard work to get to this point but they had made it.

Time seemed to pass quickly and before they knew it springtime in Iowa was upon them once more. The business was growing even larger and Tommy and Kyle was setting up locations all over the country. Ted was so very proud of them for the foresight they seemed to have for the business. When it came to construction and running one of the most prestigious companies he had ever known, his sons were naturals.

The grandchildren were growing so fast and some of them were now in school. Mandy had made her dads dream come true by accepting the job of school superintendent and was glad his prediction had come true. Even Elaine and Jerry were doing well as Ted and Sandy kept in touch with them often. As a matter of fact, the entire family had made their way back to Indiana several times and promised to continue to visit.

Spring turned into early summer and before you could blink autumn was there. Ted's favorite time of year was upon them and all the trees had already turned to the most brilliant hues of gold, orange and red. It was cool in the mornings and hot and sweltering in the afternoon. Just like Iowa is supposed to be.

Cookouts and family dinners seemed to happen nearly every weekend and everyone was the happiest they could ever remember. Football season was beginning and that meant Sunday bar-b-ques and big screen TV's. They each had their favorite teams and all of them rooted their teams to victory with a vengeance. Cheers, hollering, high fives and screams of joy were always heard from the patio on football Sunday.

Sunday was approaching and Ted knew they needed things from the supermarket. He and Sandy went to the market and packed all they could imagine needing into two overflowing grocery carts. The clerk asked if they were feeding an army as she bagged their items. They of course said it was almost like feeding an army when everyone got together at their house. They laughed and headed for home with a truckload of food.

Kyle and his family were the first to arrive, as usual. He wanted to prepare everything to perfection as he considered himself to be quite the "grill-master." Kyle would do the cooking and Tommy would watch the game and scream out highlights. It was comical and everyone always got a good laugh from those two. Kyle would cook and Tommy would shout out the play by play, what a sight.

The sun was bright and it was fast becoming a hot and sticky afternoon. A Sunday that started with heavy jackets was fast giving way to an afternoon in shirt sleeves. It was a picture perfect day and like many a Sunday spent at Ted's. Football was on two TV's and everyone was glued to one game or another. It had all the makings of a perfect family day.

After the games had ended, jabs and jeers traded, "your team lost, mine won's" exchanged, the cleaning up began. It was like any other football Sunday they had shared since the kids could remember. Everyone pitched in and helped in the cleanup and before long it was time to relax before everyone gathered their things and headed for home. Yes, just like any football Sunday they had experienced week after week. At least that's what everyone thought.

As the cleanup was done and everyone sat around exchanging small talk and relaxing before preparing to leave, Ted disappeared into the house. "Is dad all right?" Kyle asked Sandy. She said she thought so as he hadn't said anything to her before going into the house.

All three of the kids agreed that something was going on. He loved spending all the time he could with them and the kids after the cleanup was done. They couldn't see him just going in the house like that without saying anything to anyone.

As Kyle and Tommy were doing their famous rock, paper, scissors act to see who got the pleasure of going in to check on dad, Ted reappeared. He seemed to be nervous about something and was sweating. "Are you all right dad?" Mandy asked as he emerged from the house. He assured them all he was fine and said he just had to go in and get something before they all left. It was then he did something none of them ever expected, including him.

He walked over to where Sandy was sitting and knelt down beside her. He took her hand in his and looked deep into her eyes. Before Ted could open his mouth and say a word everyone was on their feet, forming a semicircle behind Sandy. As Ted opened his mouth Mandy gasped and ever so softly said "oh my God." Kyle and Tommy looked at her dazed and confused and could only whisper "what?"

It was at that very moment Mandy knew exactly what her father was about to do. She whispered to Tommy and Kyle "dad is going to propose to Sandy" and tears filled her eyes. Tommy and Kyle too had tears in their eyes, tears of joy and happiness for their dad. He of all people deserved to be happy and they just knew that Sandy was the person to do it. Ted took a deep breath and started.

"Sandy, I was lost and alone in this world and thought I was destined to be that way forever." "You came back into my life and showed me that there was not only hope but showed me that love could once again find me." "I love you with all my heart and soul and always will." "Would you make me the happiest man in the world by marrying me?" he finished as tears streamed down his face.

Before anyone could say a word, including Sandy, he pulled out a box and opened it. There inside was the most beautiful diamond ring any of them had ever seen before. Ted took the ring from the box and handed it to Sandy. Her eyes full of tears, she slid the ring on her finger and stood up. She took both his hands in hers and gently pulled him up to join her. She then jumped into his arms and screamed as loud as she could "yes, yes, yes, my God yes."

She hugged him tight and kissed him deep and continued. "You have no idea how many times I've dreamed of this day since we were kids Ted." "I was beginning to think that it would never come then you came back into my life." "I would be honored to share the rest of my life with you." Now everyone there was in tears and hugging each other tightly. The kids had prayed their dad would find happiness like this again in his life and were just glad that they were there to share the moment with him.

Mandy cried as she hugged her dad tightly and said, "daddy I'm so glad you found happiness again, you deserve it and I love you so very much." He hugged her tight as tears streamed down his face onto hers and he whispered "I love you too baby girl, I love you too, thanks for never giving up on me." "I would never give up on you daddy, you never gave up on me, ever" she said.

Tommy and Kyle took turns hugging Sandy and spinning the poor woman around like a tilt-a-whirl. Of course it was easy for them as they both stood over six foot and she was barely over five feet herself. She almost looked helpless, but very, very happy.

Ted and Mandy could only laugh as they turned and saw the sight. "Hey you two, don't break my new mom" Mandy scolded them. "Sorry sis" they said in unison and hung their heads. Of course they couldn't keep a straight face while they did, but it was the thought that counted right?

Tommy and Kyle ran over to their dad and hugged him tight. "We are so very happy for you dad" they both said. All three of the men had tears in their eyes and Ted told his sons he couldn't have gotten through all of this without them. It was the perfect ending to a night they would all remember the rest of their lives. As everyone said their goodnights and I love you's, congratulations were once again expressed to their dad and new mom.

As each left Ted and Sandy both received "I love you mom, I love you dad and I love you grandma and grandpa" from all. Sandy told them that they had no idea how good that sounded and she hoped they never got tired of saying it. "She doesn't know this family very well does she?" asked Tommy. "She'll learn quickly enough" Kyle said as they hugged them both and left.

"What exactly does that mean?" Sandy asked Ted as they went into the living room and sat on the couch together. Ted explained to her that he had always taught his kids to express their feelings openly and I love you had been a big part of their vocabularies since they were babies. "They will never get tired of saying it because they never got tired of hearing it" he told her. She said she knew they all had a special bond and could now understand why.

She like Ted grew up in a home full of love, it was just never openly or verbally expressed. You just knew that your parents loved you. They didn't actually have to say it. She was so very glad that Ted had raised his kids like he had and was never afraid to tell them just how he felt. She always knew he was a special man, she just never knew how special until this moment.

That night they went to sleep wrapped tightly in each others arms, not unlike any other night since she had moved in. Tonight though it took on new meaning. It suddenly seemed that everything wrong in the world had miraculously been made right. That all their doubts and fears of an uncertain future didn't matter anymore. It seemed that guards were finally let down completely and a trust unlike anything either of them had ever experienced had been formed. If either of them ever had any doubts of their future, tonight those doubts disappeared forever.

Chapter 21

Fall gave way to winter and soon everything was blanketed in white. It was spectacular and had almost a heavenly appearance. Christmas was a busy time this year, the house was full of family and kids and Sandy finally knew what having a family of her own really felt like. It was the best time she could ever remember having. She finally felt like she belonged somewhere and it made her feel complete. The empty spot she had felt before had been filled with love and family and she couldn't have been happier.

Christmas cookies, Christmas carols, snowball fights, building snowmen and eggnog. Sandy enjoyed every minute of it and she enjoyed it with kids and grandchildren and suddenly she knew Santa existed. He had made every Christmas wish she had ever had come true this year. She could have left this earth right then and felt complete.

Winter soon was giving way to sunshine, spring blossoms and warm southernly breezes. Ted and Sandy decided it was time to make wedding plans and wanted to include the kids in the planning. Of course Kyle and Tommy wanted a parade down Broadway and Mandy once again proved to be the logical one. She of course volunteered to take her new mom to be, shopping for a wedding dress. Ted said he should be the one to pick it out and they both said no.

Tommy and Kyle were doing their rock, paper, scissors to determine who would be the best man and it ended in a tie. Arm wrestling was suggested as a tie breaker before Ted stepped in and said he would have two best men instead of one. Of course they just looked at each other and said "wonder who the two will be?" Ted quickly smacked them both and asked if he could go dress shopping instead. Again he was told no.

Tommy and Kyle decided to get serious about their dads wedding and thought they should take Ted shopping for a tux. They told their dad that they could look good in anything but they better look far and wide to find something that could make him look good. Again they each received a smack from their dad. Once the details were worked out as to who would go shopping with whom, Ted and Sandy started making a guest list to see just how big of an event this might turn out to be.

It was soon determined that the event was going to be much bigger than his little house or yard could handle so they started looking for a place to hold their nuptials. Tommy and Kyle both lived right outside town and had more than enough room to hold the ceremony at their place. They lived next door to each other and had more than enough room. With the location decided, the guest list was once again concentrated on.

Compiling the guest list, the couple soon discovered that this was going to be quite an event after all. Since money wasn't an issue, Ted thought it best if they just catered the event. Of course Mandy jumped right in and said that she and Sandy would check out caterers and make that choice. "Besides, if it was left up to those two we would be having burgers" she said as she motioned toward her brothers.

Ted had to laugh but knew in his heart that she was probably right. "Actually, I was thinking buffalo wings and beer" Tommy piped up. He and Kyle looked at each other and shouted at the same time, "Hooters." "See what I mean?" Mandy said. Ted agreed that the wedding dress and caterer should be handled by the women.

"What's left for us to do?" Kyle asked. Again he and Tommy looked at each other, smiled and said, "bachelor party!" Ted looked so defeated and asked one more time if he could help with the dress and caterer. Again he was told no. All he could do was shake his head, look at his beaming sons, and shake his head some more.

"This is going to be interesting I can see that already" he told them all. Sandy just laughed, hugged his neck, kissed him and told him she loved him and it would be fine. "Yeah but you get the sane one" he told her. "Look at what I get stuck with" he said as he pointed to the boys. Again she just couldn't help laughing as she looked at them. They were doing their level best to put on their best innocent act and it was not working very well.

Soon wedding plans were well under way and everyone was busy. The boys surprised Ted by being on their best behavior and helping him in every way they could. They found tuxes for all the men in the wedding party and before they knew it everyone had been in for fittings. It was going to be one of the best days in Ted and Sandy's lives and they knew it would just be perfect in every way.

Mandy helped Sandy pick out a wedding dress that they both knew would make Ted's legs weak. She was so beautiful when she tried it on and Mandy couldn't help but cry when she saw her. They checked out caterers and soon had one picked out they thought was capable of meeting all their requests. It was going to be a glorious day for the couple and Mandy was just glad that her dad and Sandy had let her be a big part of it.

Ted of course asked several of the men that used to be on his crew to stand up with him and they said yes before he completely asked. They had been good friends through it all with him. His accident, his recovery and his breakup with Elaine. They had weathered all the storms with him and never once turned their backs on him or judged. He was lucky to have friends like these and he was happy they said yes when he asked them.

He and Sandy soon had the guest list completed and had the invitations ordered. Mandy helped with everything she could and soon her and Sandy were shopping almost daily. Sandy was happy to have her help and was amazed at her exquisite taste in everything. This would be a day that she would remember her entire life and she owed a bit part of that to her new stepdaughter Mandy.

They decided on a June wedding as it gave them a little more than two months to prepare everything. Kyle and Tommy had been great as well and Ted soon found that he could not only count on them if he needed them but could rely on them as well. He always knew he could, they just tend to be the rambunctious little boys he loves so much at times and it is a bit unnerving.

As plans progressed and the date neared, Tommy and Kyle

brought up something that had completely slipped Ted's mind. In all the confusion, Ted had overlooked any details for a honeymoon of any kind. How in the world could he overlook something like that he thought to himself? Kyle and Tommy sat down with their dad and went over every destination they could think of that would be a "fairytale" honeymoon.

While all their suggestions were very good ones, Ted just wasn't sure where to take Sandy. He knew that he hadn't been very far in the world, as a matter if fact, he hadn't been out of Iowa too many times. And he knew that trips to Indiana didn't count. It was hard for him to think on a worldly scale as Iowa didn't have many honeymoon spots that he could recall.

There was a place that Ted had always dreamed of visiting if he ever had the means to do it. He just wasn't sure that it would be fair to Sandy to take her there. It was Kyle that put his hand on his dads shoulder and asked, "what's wrong dad?" As he looked at his sons, he could see the concern on both their faces. He quickly told them it was really nothing to be concerned about.

He told the boys that he had always wanted to go to Hawaii but didn't know if it would be fair to take Sandy there. "Why wouldn't it be fair to Sandy dad?" Tommy had to ask. "Hawaii is where I always wanted to take your mom if we ever got the money to go" he told his boys. "I just don't know if it would be right to take Sandy there now" he went on.

The boys both assured him that there wouldn't be anything unfair about it as his dream destination had never worked out with mom anyway. "I don't think anyone would ever give it a second thought dad" Tommy told him. "Besides dad, why don't we all just keep this our little secret" Kyle added. Ted knew he was right and told his sons that it would remain between just them.

The boys finally convinced him that just because he had always wanted to take their mom there, he and mom weren't together anymore either. That shouldn't stop him from taking Sandy there and having the time of their lives they told him. He knew in his heart they were right, his head just told him it was a bad idea. He decided to listen to his heart for once and asked them when they got so wise and smart. They said they even amazed themselves at times.

Before he could change his mind a dozen times, they were making reservations and booking flights. Only after the boys had everything confirmed and paid for did they tell their dad of the trip. They were not going to take any chances that he would back out at the last minute. The rest of the wedding plans went smoothly and before they knew it, everything was done.

The cake had been picked out and ordered, tuxes were ordered and had been fitted. The caterer was booked and Sandy's dress was picked out and had been fitted. Invitations were ordered and mailed and the honeymoon was booked and paid for. The wedding day was fast approaching but they were all ready for it.

Tommy and Kyle had everything ready at their homes for not only the wedding but the reception as well. They knew their dad and Sandy both loved country music and even booked a very good local country band for the reception. It would be a day to remember and all his children could be proud of themselves for the job they all did in helping to make this day happen.

Of course they did it out of love and devotion to their dad but they also did it because they only wanted to see him happy again. They all knew that Sandy would make that happen and loved her with all their hearts for that. All three of them watched their dad go to pieces after their mom did what she did. Sandy had been the answer to their prayers as they only wanted their dad to be happy and she makes him happy.

With the wedding right around the corner they all checked and double checked every last detail. They didn't want any unexpected surprises coming up at the last minute and the kids were great. Each of them had a list of calls to make to check and recheck everything. Only after Mandy was satisfied that nothing could go wrong did they breathe easier. She was like a drill sergeant when she wanted to be, and when it came to her dads wedding, she was the toughest.

Mandy even called her mom and asked if they would return the favor and attend dads wedding. Of course Elaine said she and Jerry would be there front and center just like they all had done for her. They talked about all the details and Elaine secretly helped with some last minute overlooked things. Mandy was glad she still had mom to call at times like this.

Soon everything really was done and had been triple checked. The RSVP's were flooding in and final counts on how many would attend were being passed on to the florist and caterer. Although they could all breath a little easier, Mandy wasn't about to let down her guard just yet. She was more than prepared should anything come up at the last minute and everyone was praying it didn't. "God help the person that calls her with a problem now" Kyle told them.

It was kind of funny to think about, but they all knew he was right. She would be someone's worst nightmare if they approached her with a problem at this point Ted thought. He smiled to himself as he couldn't help but think that she had inherited her moms temper at times like this.

He hadn't really allowed thoughts of Elaine to enter his mind during all of this. That kind of surprised him even after the talk they had before he asked Sandy to marry him. He knew that Elaine only wanted him to be happy and move forward with his life.

He had finally come to a point in his life where he could think about her and still have the courage to move on and concentrate on being happy for himself. All the thoughts of the past and what had happened between them had been buried and put to rest once and for all, finally. It was a big step for him but one he knew in his heart he had to make. Sandy was his future and he couldn't wait to begin a brand-new life with her. He finally knew that he deserved it.

That was something he never would have admitted a few short years ago. Now he was not only willing to admit it, but he honestly believed it. As he looked back at all the things that had happened he was finally ready to let go, really let go. Elaine was the past and we can't live in the past or dwell on it. It only brings us sorrow and heartache. Sandy was his future and his future was now bright and full of promise and joy.

He had lived in the past long enough and knew that it was time to stop. He was getting more than a little nervous at the thought of starting another new life but knew this time he wouldn't be doing it alone. It would be another new start that would last him and Sandy both an entire lifetime. It would be a start they would make together. He liked the sound of that. They would do it together. That sounded so good to him, it sounded so right.

Chapter 22

The sun was bright, the wind was nothing more than a whisper and the day was picture perfect in every way. It was their wedding day. It had finally arrived and everyone had remained safe. Only because no one went to Mandy with problems or last minute changes or cancellations. Ted and the boys were already in their tuxes and looked so handsome. They were all meeting guests as they arrived and were seated.

Mandy was the only one allowed to see Sandy before she made that final walk down that aisle toward her dad. Tommy and Kyle had tried to run some reconnaissance for their dad but were met by Sergeant Mandy in the process. Both boys told him that they would never make that mistake again. They had always kind if underestimated their sister, but not today.

The guests were seated and Ted and the rest of his wedding party had taken their positions in the front. As Ted turned to take one last look over the crowd, he noticed something he hadn't noticed until now. Elaine was sitting there in the front row and she was positively beaming. This made him a bit uneasy but the boys just hugged him and told him she wanted to be there. "It's going to be fine dad" they both told him.

He knew his sons were right. He had been there for her when she married the last time. Deep down inside he was glad she could be here to support him and Sandy today. He smiled and simply mouthed the words "thank you." The sound of the wedding march brought him back to reality and he looked to see the most beautiful, breathtaking sight he had ever seen before in his life standing there waiting to join him.

Sandy looked absolutely heavenly and the entire crowd gasped as they too turned to see her. Mandy had outdone herself and soon this captivating woman would be his wife. He knew at that minute he was the luckiest man in the world and always would be. Sandy was simply glowing and could have lit up the entire world at that very minute.

Her lifelong dream of marrying her childhood sweetheart would come true today. It would be the best day of her life and a day she never thought would come to be.

The ceremony was spectacular and went off without a hitch. The kids had all done a wonderful job in all they did to help make this day happen. Sandy and Ted couldn't be happier and even Sandy was glad to see that Elaine and her husband had made it. Today she didn't feel threatened or uneasy with Elaine's presence. She was just happy she had come to support Ted as he did her a short time ago. Yes, today was the most perfect day Sandy could ever remember and she only hoped it never ended.

The festivities went well into the night and soon people were saying their goodbyes and congratulations. Ted and Sandy met each and everyone and said thank you for coming. It was indeed the perfect ending to a perfect day.

Mandy, Kyle and Tommy were so happy for their dad and new step mother. It was plain to see that today he had allowed himself the luxury of being completely and selflessly happy and put the past to rest finally.

Elaine and Jerry stayed with Kyle and soon all the guests had either left or were leaving. Ted and Sandy were ready to collapse from all the activity and Sandy knew Ted would need to sit down soon. He had been on his feet all day and she knew that was hard on his knees. Mandy had filled her in on his condition and warned her that he would overdo it if she allowed him to. She watched him like a hawk and knew it was time to get him off his feet for a while.

She quickly enlisted Tommy and Kyle to help her get him in a chair and to keep him there for a while. Tommy suggested duct tape and Kyle never missed a beat by starting the rock, paper, scissors thing to see who would hold him down. Tommy lost.

Ted knew that it was time to sit down and take it easy for a while. His knees were telling him this and he knew he overdid it a bit today. He would pay for it tomorrow but today he just wanted everything to be perfect for Sandy. He soon found a somewhat comfortable chair and sat down. It felt good to get off his feet for a while and give his poor legs, feet and knees a much needed rest.

As he sat and reflected on the day, he was happy that everyone had made it to the wedding. He got to see old friends that he hadn't seen in a while. Men that used to be on his crew and were now his employees and their families had come. Even his old boss and his family came and he was so thrilled to see them all. Friends from his neighborhood that had watched him build the life he has today were there and if the ceremony had been held in town, even more would have come he was sure.

For the moment, he was glad it was over, excited about he and Sandy leaving in the morning for their honeymoon and thankful for all those that had shared this special day with them. He was even happy that Elaine had come. He briefly thought about asking her but wasn't sure if that would be right or not. He was just glad that she made it and shared his joy and happiness today as he had done for her not long ago.

He was brought back to the moment by the sound of chairs being pulled up beside him. He noticed that the only people still there were his children and their families, Elaine and Jerry and Sandy. They sat and talked about how beautiful Sandy looked and how everyone just fell in love with her dress. The men talked about how good the food had been and agreed that the band was excellent.

The women talked about flowers, dresses and the overall success of the day and the men could only think of their stomachs. They all discussed plans for the cleanup and everyone pledged to pitch in and help the next day. They all decided the mess could wait till morning as they were all exhausted from a very busy and full day.

Ted said that he and Sandy would stop by in the morning and help before they left. Of course his children wouldn't hear of that and told him to stay away until they returned from their honeymoon. Mandy said to make sure he brought plenty of pictures and had a few suggestions for thank you gifts.

He promised they would have lots of pictures and would bring souvenirs for everyone. They exchanged hugs, kisses, thank you's, I love you's and goodnights before Ted and Sandy left. Mandy hugged her dad and told him that she was happier than words could say for the both of them. He knew that his daughter had always wanted him to be happy and would have moved heaven and earth to see it happen for him.

He thanked each of his children and told them how very much he loved them before they left. He even went over to Elaine and thanked her and Jerry for sharing this special day with he and Sandy and hugged her tight. He knew that this would be one of the last times he would see her in a very long time and the closure was one he needed yet regretted.

Everyone had tears in their eyes that night. Some were tears of joy and some were tears of sorrow in a way. It was the final chapter in a life that started years ago with a pregnant girlfriend and ended tonight with her remaining just a friend. She had been his entire life for so long and tonight he started fresh. He started over.

Ted had booked the honeymoon suite at one of the better hotels in town and soon he and Sandy slipped away for their first night together as man and wife. Everyone waved as they drove away and they all just knew that their dad would be fine now. It made them so very happy to see that he had moved on. A bit of sadness also came over them as they looked and saw their mom standing there waving goodbye with tears streaming down her face.

Even though she had been the one to make that fateful decision to move on with her life with another all those years ago, they knew it still had to be tearing her apart inside to watch him leave. Elaine knew that this would be the last time she would see Ted in a long time and that saddened her as well. She would always love him and could only wish now that she had listened to him when he said he wanted to work things out between them.

It was now a decision she would have to live with the rest of her life. Not that she didn't love the man she was married to now, she did. She loved him with all her heart. It just tore her up to think now that she had made the life altering mistake years ago not to work things out with Ted. And, she knew this was the end of the story for her and Ted. Once he made his mind up to do something as big as he had today, he would never change his mind. No matter what.

Elaine knew that should her marriage end tomorrow, she would spend the rest of her life alone because Ted wasn't the kind of man to leave Sandy for another chance with her. Not now, not after she had told him to move on. She meant every word she had told him just a short time ago when he called. He deserved to be happy and she knew that now he was. That didn't ease the pain she was feeling at that moment but she knew she would be fine as well, they both would.

Ted was old-fashioned and was not about to let Sandy walk into the room that night. As soon as the door swung open, he picked her up in his arms and carried her through. She was floating on a cloud that night and hoped the feeling would never end. She had loved this man her entire life and never thought this day would be anything but a dream. If this was a dream, she did not want to wake up.

Although she had repeatedly asked Ted where they would be spending their honeymoon, he would only say, "you'll see." She had guessed and guessed and found that he wasn't about to tell her even if she had guessed right.

Little did she know that she hadn't even came close but Ted just knew she would be thrilled when they arrived. They would leave tomorrow morning and be there by tomorrow night. He could barely wait to see her face when they stepped off the plane that next night.

Ted was not usually the romantic type but he had managed to arrange for fresh roses to be delivered to the room and they were everywhere. As soon as they were inside and had looked around a bit Sandy noticed a warm bath had already been drawn. Rose petals were scattered about everywhere, and candles flickered ever so softly giving the room a heaven glow. He had thought of everything, including a bottle of champaign chilling in the ice bucket.

As they looked about, Ted was suddenly proud of himself. He

really had done an outstanding job for not knowing what he was doing. Soon they were buried in bubbles and sipping champaign. It was the perfect end to a day that would last forever. Or at least Sandy thought it was the perfect end, she had no idea that in his mind this was just the beginning of their night.

That night they tossed all their inhibitions out the window and made love so wildly and loudly the front desk actually called twice and asked if they could keep it down. They both laughed and said they would try.

It was the perfect night and the first night in the beginning of a life that would last forever. They became one soul that night and couldn't have been happier. Ted just knew that all the twists and turns he had taken to get to this point were for a reason. He was happy for the first time in a very long time and loved the feeling.

They slept in the next morning and nearly missed breakfast. Ted woke first and ordered room service. The knock on the door told him that breakfast was being served and he signed the ticket, tipped the man and pulled the cart inside. He went to his sleeping bride and woke her with a passionate kiss and an I love you. She thought she had died and went to heaven.

After breakfast they took turns showering and gathered their things to leave. Ted called the kids and each one said they would miss them both and to have a good trip. Kyle said him and Tommy would pick up his truck from the airport and take it to his house. Kyle said to call before they landed and he would either meet them or have someone there to pick them up.

They quickly checked their boarding passes and found seats and settled in. "Are you finally going to tell me where we are going?" Sandy asked her new husband. He told her again, "you'll see" and left it at that. She could have choked him if she didn't love him so much. Wherever it was, she just knew she would love it and it would be perfect. Since she was till wore out from the night before, she quickly put on her earphones and turned on some light music.

Before takeoff she was sound asleep and Ted was having trouble staying awake as well. The flight was only making one stop and then it would be on to Hawaii nonstop. He was glad they didn't have to spend the night somewhere as he really wanted to get there and have the flight behind them. Jet lag was no fun and he was sure they would want to rest that first night.

Soon they were landing and the flight attendant was waking them. She told them it would be a while before they took off again. They both stretched, yawned and rubbed their eyes. "Are we there yet?" she managed to mumble. Ted playfully swatted her bottom and told her to get up and they would go find some much needed coffee. The stop seemed short and before they realized it they were taking off again. The next stop would be their final destination for two whole weeks.

Chapter 23

They landed in the middle of the night and Ted was grateful for that. They both were so wore out they barely noticed the Leigh that was placed around each of their necks as they walked wearily toward the airport entrance. Ted had arranged to have a limo pick them up and was glad it was waiting for them. He didn't have the energy or patience right now to wait for it.

They were quickly seated in the back and the driver loaded their bags in the trunk. Soon they were being whisked off to their hotel and would sleep late in the morning. He was almost certain of that. They arrived at the motel quickly and were in their room before they knew it. All they had the energy to do was undress and climb into bed and collapse again.

Ted was the first to wake the next morning. He was slow in the rising part but he did wake first. Sandy was still sleeping peacefully beside him and he just didn't have the heart to wake her. He quickly went to his bags and searched for his pain pills. Although the flight was first class and very luxurious, it lacked in enough leg room for him and his knees were letting him know it this morning.

He cleared his head, found his pain pills, took one and headed straight for the shower. Thinking it best to get his out of the way now as he knew that Sandy would probably want to take a nice long hot shower when she woke. After his shower and preparations to face a new day were complete, he started a pot of coffee. He knew that Sandy would welcome a boost this morning and he was in dire need of one himself.

Just as the gurgling coffee maker stopped spitting and sputtering he poured himself a cup and walked out onto the patio. The suite they had was a ground floor room completely with their own beachfront private patio. The brochures the boys had received on it looked like a dream come true. And from what little he had seen so far, it was.

Tiptoeing in for a second cup of coffee, he was met by an absolutely stunning bride. She hugged him tight and kissed him deep and asked where in the world they were. Without saying a word he simply opened the blinds on the patio doors. She asked "is that the ocean Ted?" He could only laugh and say yes. She said that still didn't answer her question. He couldn't keep it from her any longer and told her they were in Hawaii. She actually shrieked and started jumping up and down like a little kid.

He only wanted to bring her here in hopes it would make her happy, seems that it worked he thought. During several of their talks he had discovered that like him, Sandy hadn't done much in the way of traveling. She had been further than Iowa, but not much further. Neither of them had traveled outside the United States and when asked about dream destinations, Hawaii was one of her favorites.

Even as the boys booked this trip, he had more than a little apprehension about bringing her here. Not because he didn't think she would just love it. But because it was always somewhere he had dreamed of taking Elaine if they ever had the money. Now that they were here, he could see just how foolish those thoughts were in the first place. She was so happy and more alive and excited than he could remember seeing her since they came back into each others lives.

Seeing her like this confirmed just how right he was in going ahead with his plans to bring her here. She asked if he would pour her a cup of coffee while she showered. He told her that he would order breakfast as well and did as she jumped in the shower. What he was sure would be a long relaxing shower turned into a record-breaking quickie. She was done, dressed and makeup on before their meal arrived. He was flabbergasted.

He would have bet that she would be in there an hour and here she was ready to take on the world in just minutes. She was full of surprises and each one he discovered made him love her that much more. Soon they were sitting on their patio enjoying breakfast to the sound of waves lapping the beach and seagulls crying above them. It was like something out of a movie and he was glad indeed that he chose to spend their honeymoon here.

They relaxed and planned out the rest of their day as they sipped coffee and soaked up the morning sun. It was more beautiful than either of them could have imagined and neither of them wanted it to end...ever. He called the front desk and asked if his rental car was ready. They assured him it was ready and waiting.

They decided to just take that first day to explore and do whatever they wanted. Why try to stick to some plan? They usually don't work out anyway or leave you short on time and you rush through everything. Neither of them wanted to rush and they didn't intend on missing a single thing. He told her they were there for two full weeks and intended to see everything, do everything and go everywhere. He told her they had time to take their time.

She liked the sound of that and had hoped he would want to take their time and see as much as they could while they were there. Besides, Sandy wasn't sure if or when they might ever come back and wanted to try to do it all now. She was like a little kid in a toy store with a handful of money right before Christmas. She wanted it all and wanted it now.

That first day they took their time. They drove along the beach. They found some quaint shops and had to buy souvenirs for everyone. Mountains, waterfalls, volcanoes and palm trees were everywhere and they took in each and every sight. Their poor digital camera was getting the workout of its life today he thought as she snapped picture after picture. They ate lunch and found a place to print the pictures they had taken so far.

Pictures didn't really do this place justice but the ones she had taken were breathtaking. They knew the kids would love to see each one. After lunch they did some more sightseeing and shopping before returning to their room. It was fast approaching evening and they had crammed a lot into one day as it was. They ate dinner in the restaurant at the motel and it was all she could have hoped for.

After dinner they went for a moonlight stroll along the beach and it was beyond description. He held her in his arms and kissed her under the star filled sky. "I love you so very much" he told her as they sat and just listened to the waves. Neither of them wanted this night to end but they both were still a bit weary from the flight. They walked back to their room, made love and fell asleep wrapped tightly in each others arms. It was a dream come true for both of them.

Morning seemed to come quickly but was welcomed with a newfound anticipation. They both had slept well and were rested and ready to face a new day. Sandy put on a pot of coffee as Ted showered. He soon had company. After their shower, they took their coffee onto the patio and fell in love with the place all over again. They quickly ordered breakfast and knew they had to call the kids and let them know they were fine.

Mandy was the first call they made as they knew she would be the one to pace the floor until she heard from them. She was excited to here from them and had to let the children talk to grandpa and grandma before she hung up.

They knew they could catch both boys at the office so they called there next. The boys too were excited to hear from them and happy they were enjoying themselves. They told them they loved them and to hurry home before ending the call.

Sandy was now ready to take on the world. She had breakfast behind her, coffee to wake her up and refresh her and had spoke to her step children and grandchildren. She was now complete and ready for another fun filled day of sightseeing. Ted quickly downed his coffee, grabbed his jacket and followed her out the door.

The next two weeks were full and rewarding and they did everything they set out to do. They visited all the Islands and saw all the attractions. They had a wonderful time but were both ready to go home and see the kids and grandchildren. Since this would be their last night here, they enjoyed dinner in their room. They ate on the patio and took one last moonlit walk on the beach.

They had the beach to themselves and decided to take advantage of the situation. That night they made love on the beach under the stars as the warm ocean water washed over them with each wave. It was the kind of night that fairytales are written about and they were happy they took such a risky chance. "If the kids knew, they would be mortified" Sandy told him. Ted assured her that the boys would be ok with it and think they were "cool" for doing it.

Morning would again feel as though it came much too quickly and this time they were not looking forward to their day. They would be leaving today and the flight home would again be tiring and long. As Ted showered, Sandy made coffee and ordered breakfast. They enjoyed one last meal on their patio and watched the waves lazily lap the shore. The sky was blue, sun was bright, sand on the beach was as white as snow and the water was the most spectacular shade of blue. It was unlike anyplace either of them had ever seen before.

After breakfast, they packed and made one last check of the room to ensure they weren't forgetting anything before heading for the front desk to check out. Their flight was a somewhat early one and they would be back home before it got too late. Soon they were on their way to the airport and boarding their return flight before they knew it. Neither of them wanted to leave but they both knew it was time to go home. They missed the kids and couldn't wait to see them.

The flight home was long and exhausting and they couldn't wait to sleep in their own bed tonight. Kyle picked them up at the airport and drove them home. He asked how the trip was and knew they both were tired when they just said fine.

He also knew that none of them would hear from these two too early tomorrow. After carrying their bags in the house he hugged them both, told them it was good to have them home and told them to go to bed. They did just as they were told and told him they loved him before he left.

As expected they both slept in the next morning and wouldn't have minded if they spent the entire day in bed. Neither of them was about to do that though. They had missed the kids and grandchildren so much they couldn't wait to see them. As soon as they were fully awake and moving they called and arranged to meet them for dinner at one of their favorite restaurants. The kids said they couldn't wait to see them and a time was agreed on to meet.

They spent the rest of the day unpacking, putting things away and sorting out pictures and gifts they had brought back. The day quickly got away from them and dinner time was fast approaching. They gathered everything and headed for the restaurant.

As they entered, they were quickly mobbed by screaming grandchildren and exchanged hugs and I love you's. Mandy hugged them both and told them how much she missed them. Kyle and Tommy were next in line and soon they were being shown to their table.

As soon as they had ordered Sandy started taking out envelope after envelope of pictures. They were passed around and everyone thought they were beautiful. Of course the grandchildren were only interested in knowing if they brought them anything.

They all laughed and Ted assured them that they had something for everyone. After dinner they laughed and talked about all the wonderful things they had seen and done. The kids were happy their dad decided to go after all.

Gifts were passed out and everyone just loved what they got. Soon it was time for everyone to say goodnight and head for home. Ted and Sandy were happy to be home, sad to leave such a wondrous place and anxious to settle into a routine as man and wife. Life was good and it only seemed it would get better. They exchanged hugs, kisses, I love you's and goodnights before each going their separate ways.

<u>Chapter 24</u>

Days turned into weeks, weeks turned into months and before they knew it a year had already passed. Ted and Sandy were planning a dinner for the family to help them celebrate their first anniversary and they couldn't be happier. The business had grown even more in the last year and Ted was nothing but a name on the letterhead. He had retired completely after he and Sandy married so he could spend every minute with the woman he loved.

Sandy got closer and closer to the kids and grandchildren and they all loved her dearly. The last year found Ted and Sandy doing something else they never saw themselves doing. They traveled all over the country seeing sights they had always wanted to see but never took the initiative to do before. They were inseparable and loved each other like there would be no tomorrow.

With the return of each trip came dinners with kids, gifts for everyone and pictures to share. Tommy and Kyle had now grown the business to be one of the largest in the country and Ted couldn't be happier or prouder of them. Mandy was now in charge of the entire school district and everyone just loved the job she was doing. She was a natural and Ted always knew she would go far.

Sandy couldn't be prouder of them all or love them any more if she had been their birth mother. She was a proud mom indeed and never passed up an opportunity to brag about her kids to anyone that would listen. Ted learned that Elaine and Jerry had started a little business of their own and it was doing magnificently.

He learned that Elaine had remembered the money Ted had put in savings for her when she first moved to Indiana. She had completely forgotten about it and wanted to put it to good use. So, her and Jerry used that money to open their new business and it was doing great. He was so happy that she finally found her place in life and a person to share it with her.

Memories of her still wound their way in and out of Ted's thoughts and probably always would. He was finally comfortable with that and accepted it. Holidays and special gatherings still found Elaine and Jerry joining them and Elaine was genuinely happy for Ted and Sandy. She was glad they had found each other again and eventually her and Sandy became very close friends.

Ted and the boys still spent "football Sunday" together with the rest of the family. Cookouts and TV were still the order of the day and even Sandy had adopted a favorite team and could be found yelling above the rest rooting them on. Yes life had finally come full circle for Ted. He was happy with his life and devoted to Sandy like no man anyone knew. They complimented each other perfectly and all that knew them, knew they would be the couple to last all eternity.

The grandchildren were all in school now and everyone was growing up or growing older. Ted and Sandy still acted like highschool sweethearts and didn't think they would ever grow up. Ted learned that Sandy had an undisclosed passion for classic cars in that first year and they actually bought and restored several together. The kids thought it was great that they had an interest they could share and a passion and love they could work on together.

Tommy and Kyle both bought cars they had restored and just knew that their mom and dad could start another successful business if they chose to. At times they would travel the old countryside's of Iowa looking in old barns and in fields for their next project. They loved their outings and usually found something to restore or something for parts. The kids had never seen anything like it.

Sandy and Elaine actually spent hours on the phone and became the very best of friends. That was something Ted had never thought he would see. The two of them actually becoming friends.

They did though and soon they talked almost daily. Even the kids were happy that their two moms were friends. They loved them both and didn't ever want to be put in the position of choosing between them. When they became friends, the kids couldn't have been happier.

Life was good for this family and Ted had finally put the ghosts of the past to rest and found love again. Sandy was the best thing to happen to him, he only wished he could have seen that years ago. In some way he still felt a bit cheated that he had missed all those years away from her.

Maybe he should have just stood up to Elaine's mom all those years ago and followed his heart instead. As he looks back though, he wouldn't have done anything any differently. He would have missed having three wonderful children and couldn't imagine his life without them in it. He finally decided that life had worked out just like it was supposed to do and he was content with that.

No matter what had happened in the past, he and Sandy had the brightest of futures now and that was all that really mattered in the end. They had found their way back to each other through all the heartache and mishaps and knew they were together to stay this time. With each passing day life only got better and they only got closer. It was like falling in love with her all over again each and every day and Ted loved the feeling.

He couldn't think of life without Sandy in it and knew that could only mean this was real love. Sandy was like no other woman he had ever known and so different from when they were kids. He thanked God each and every day for blessing him with such a wonderful woman. He didn't know this at the time, but Sandy too thanked God for allowing him to find his way back into her life as well.

The years were passing rapidly and Ted and Sandy watched as their children matured and grew and their grandchildren became young adults. They still traveled as often as they could and continued to work on cars as they felt like it. Life was still full for them and one of the grandchildren always had something for them to attend. School plays, soccer, softball, you name it. They were front and center right beside the kids cheering loud enough to be heard above the crowd.

Of course most of the time the only voice you could hear was Sandy. She had grown so much in the last few years and her life was now full and had purpose. Ted had only learned recently that she had always felt a bit cheated from not having children of her own. She confessed it to him on one of their outings scouting for cars and parts. She also told him that his kids had filled a big void in her life by accepting and loving her like they had.

He never wanted her to feel like she had missed out on anything but knew that children at this point in their lives would pretty much be out of the question. She assured him that she had no intentions of becoming a mother in any capacity other than being mom to his kids. She was more than happy to settle for that and her life was now full and meaningful. He was glad to hear her say that as he really didn't want to think about four a.m. feedings and dirty diapers. As they look back on it now, they laugh and think how silly that sounded.

The city was growing and Kyle and Tommy were building much of it or involved in the process in one way or another. Mandy has watched as new schools sprang up within the community and her job has taken on new meaning and more responsibility. The grandchildren were getting older and would soon be thinking or driving and dating. Times Ted could remember well and dreaded the thought even now. Life was good for the family and everyone had their health.

Ted and Sandy would reflect back over the last few years with no regrets or disappointments. They had a full and rewarding life and things only seemed to get better with time. They had their moments like any couple but always went to bed laughing and loving. They were the kind of couple others want to be like and few would accomplish. Mandy, Kyle and Tommy all only hoped they could remain as happy as their dad was now. They worked hard and loved even harder and had learned so very much from this man.

Yes life was good and only getting better and in the end, they all learned one thing for sure. Never give up on love and happiness because it will find you somehow, someway. Always follow your heart because your head might not always know what's right for you in the end. Always put family first and love like there is no tomorrow. Do this and you'll be as happy as Ted and Sandy. The kids are all following their lead and everyone will live happily ever after.

About The Book

All we hear about today is how the "scorned woman" survives a terrible relationship to rebuild her life and carry on alone. We seldom ever hear about the "scorned man" and how he had a woman that cheated on him, broke his heart and left him alone. In "For Better, For Worse??" we find our character Ted alone and starting life over after his wife of over 25 years is caught cheating on him.

Follow this mans journey as he struggles to cope with his new life, tries to make sense of what his ex did to him and watch as he rebuilds life from the ground up....alone. Watch as he finds peace with the past, learns to trust again and if at all possible, love once more. It is a touching story from a mans point of view and needs to be told.

We cheer and applaud when a woman rebuilds her life after a cheating man breaks her heart. Give this man a standing ovation as he shoulders the blame for their breakup so she can save face with everyone and builds a life he can be proud of. You will laugh, cry, get angry, cheer him on....you'll run the emotional gauntlet and want more. It's a romance with a twist and is ahead of it's time.

About The Author

The author is a 50-year-old husband, father of three, and Grandfather of Five, with number six due in March of 2006, that finds himself disabled due to a 3rd time back injury. Unable to work, and nothing but time on his hands, he decided to take an English Comp teachers advise, write.

His first attempt to write anything other than business proposals and book reports, was his first book *"Bridges Revisited"* and it was released in 2003. The author released his second book titled *"Winter Roses"* in the spring of 2005. Not fully satisfied with the first edition of *"Bridges Revisited"* he released a *Revised Edition* of that book in January of 2006. This is his third book to date and he admits number four and five are already in the works as well. This book titled *"For Better, For Worse??"* is one he feels is his best yet.

Like *"Bridges Revisited"* the author chose Iowa as the setting for his second book as well as the third book. The third book is town specific as is *"Bridges Revisited"* and he chose the setting as Council Bluffs, Iowa. He is not only truly an Iowa author but chooses to set his books in Iowa as well. A state he is proud to call home.

Married nearly 30 years to the love of his life, Vicki, they have three children. A daughter Randi, their oldest, is married with three children of her own and lives in Iowa as well. Their middle child, the oldest boy, Kelly Jr., is still single and currently lives in Wichita, Kansas, and hopes to relocate there permanently with his long time girlfriend after she graduates nursing school in 2006. The youngest, their son Carl, is currently serving in the United States Air Force and stationed at McConnell Air Force Base in Wichita, Kansas. Carl was married last year and his wife Jeci has two girls with a new baby boy due in March of 2006. Carl has served in Iraq and in January of 2006 went to Kuwait for four months. The author and his wife Vicki are extremely proud of all their children.

Printed in the United States
50867LVS00002B/22-33

9 780976 626046